He was just about to say goodbye and send Catherine on her way when she eased forward, rose on tiptoe and lifted her lips to kiss him goodbye.

Of course.

Great idea.

There was an audience present, and they were two people in love. A goodbye kiss was definitely in order.

Ray stepped in and lowered his mouth to hers, but as their lips met, he found himself wrapping his arms around her and pulling her close, savoring the feel of her in his arms, the scent of her shampoo, the taste of her....

Oh, wow.

Dear Reader,

If you're like me, you enjoy a marriage—or engagement—of convenience story. And when that story is set in a small Texas town, with cowboys and ranchers and babies… Well, you have all the fixings for a great romance.

So welcome back to Brighton Valley, where interim mayor and wealthy rancher Ray Mendez has more money and property than he can shake a stick at—even after a lengthy legal battle with his gold-digging ex-wife. Now that the divorce is final, every single woman in town is determined to win his battered heart. But Ray's not interested.

When he meets visiting actress and dancer Catherine Loza, he hires her to be his pretend fiancée to keep the women at bay until his interim position as mayor is finished. The scheme works beautifully—until Ray finds it difficult to draw the line at playacting, and Catherine realizes her temporary gig just might be the role of a lifetime.

So I hope you'll pack this book in your suitcase—or take it down to the shore or the pool with you—for some good summer reading.

Wishing you romance,

Judy

THE RANCHER'S HIRED FIANCÉE

JUDY DUARTE

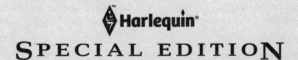

Recycling programs
for this product may
not exist in your area.

ISBN-13: 978-0-373-65675-2

THE RANCHER'S HIRED FIANCÉE

Recent books by Judy Duarte

JUDY DUARTE

always knew there was a book inside her, but since English was her least-favorite subject in school, she never considered herself a writer. An avid reader who enjoys a happy ending, Judy couldn't shake the dream of creating a book of her own.

Her dream became a reality in March 2002, when Silhouette Special Edition released her first book, *Cowboy Courage*. Since then she has published more than twenty novels.

Her stories have touched the hearts of readers around the world. And in July 2005 Judy won a prestigious Readers' Choice Award for *The Rich Man's Son*.

Judy makes her home near the beach in Southern California. When she's not cooped up in her writing cave, she's spending time with her somewhat enormous but delightfully close family.

To Mark Winch, who reads every book I write.
I hope you enjoy this one, too, Mark.

Chapter One

Catherine Loza napped in a child's bedroom at the Walker family's ranch in Texas, dreaming of sold-out nights on Broadway, the heady sound of applause and the pounding of her heart after a well-executed performance.

She took a bow, then straightened and glanced out into the audience, only to see an empty stall and a bale of straw in an illuminated old barn, where a group of children clapped their hands in delight.

Their faces were a blur until two of them glided toward the stage, greeting her with red rosebuds, their long stems free of thorns.

Recognizing Sofia and Stephen, Dan and Eva Walker's youngest twins, Catherine knelt and received the flowers. Then the darling two-year-olds wrapped their pudgy arms around her and placed soft, moist kisses on her cheeks, on her forehead, on her chin.

How strange, she thought, but so sweet.

She'd no more than thanked them and sent them on their way when she heard a light tapping noise in the distance.

Thoughts and visions tumbled together in her sleepy mind—until another knock sounded, this time on the bedroom door.

"Yes?" she said, realizing she'd dozed off after reading a storybook to the children. Now, as she scanned the empty room, she saw that they'd both slipped off, leaving her to nap alone.

Eva opened the door and peered into the darkened bedroom. "I'm sorry to bother you, but we're having company for dinner tonight, and I thought you might want to know."

Catherine glanced out the window, which was shuttered tight, only a faint light creeping through the slats. She tried to guess the time of day but didn't have a clue—other than it was obviously nearing the dinner hour.

"A lot of help I am," Catherine said. "I wasn't the one who was supposed to fall asleep."

Eva chuckled softly. "Sofia and Stephen woke up a few minutes ago. Now they're in the kitchen, coloring and playing with their sticker books."

Catherine never had been one to nap during the day. Apparently the fresh air, sunshine and the rural Texas setting had a calming effect on her.

"If you'd like to rest a little longer," Eva said, "it's

not a problem. You've been burning the candle at both ends for so long. Your body probably needs the sleep."

"Who's coming for dinner tonight?" Catherine asked.

"Ray Mendez. He's a local rancher and a neighbor. In fact, he'll be here any minute."

"Thanks for the heads-up." As Eva closed the bedroom door, Catherine raked her fingers through her hair, her nails catching on a couple of snags in her long curls. She probably looked a fright, with eyes puffy from sleep, but she wouldn't stress about it. This was supposed to be a vacation of sorts.

Ever since her arrival on the ranch, she'd decided to go au natural—no makeup, no fancy hairstyles. She was also kicking back for a change—no schedules, no grueling workouts, no rehearsals. And quite frankly, she was looking forward to having a break from the hectic life she'd once known in Manhattan.

Catherine rolled to the side of the bed and got to her feet. Then she straightened the pillows, as well as the coverlet, before opening the door and stepping into the hall.

She'd taken only two steps when the doorbell rang. The rancher had just arrived. Wanting to make herself useful, she detoured to answer the door. What had Eva said his name was? Ray something.

Catherine had never met any of the Walkers' neighbors, but she assumed Ray must be one of Hank's friends. Hank, Dan's elderly uncle, who'd once owned the ranch and now lived in a guesthouse Dan had built for him, always ate dinner with them in the main dining room.

Not seeing anyone else in the room, Catherine opened the front door.

She expected to see a weathered rancher who resembled Dan's uncle, a sweet but crotchety old cowboy who reminded her of Robert Duvall when he'd played in *Lonesome Dove* or *Open Range*. But nothing had prepared her for the tall, dark-haired visitor who stood on the porch.

The man, whose expression revealed that he was just as surprised to see her as she was to see him, didn't look anything like the grizzled Texan she'd envisioned just moments before. At first glance, he bore enough resemblance to Antonio Banderas to be his younger brother—all decked out in Western wear, of course.

A sense of awkwardness rose up inside, and she tried to tamp it down the best she could. She might be dressed like a barefoot street urchin in a pair of gray sweatpants, an old NYU T-shirt and no makeup to speak of, but she was actually an accomplished woman who'd performed on Broadway several times in the past—and would do so again.

"I'm Catherine Loza," she said. "You must be Ray...?"

"Mendez." His voice held the slightest bit of a Spanish accent, which made him all the more intriguing.

She reached up to flick a wild strand of her sleep-tousled curls from her eyes, only to feel something papery stuck to her face. She peeled it off, and when she looked at her fingers to see what it was, she spotted a child's butterfly sticker.

Oh, for Pete's sake. How had that gotten there?

It must have been on the bedspread or pillow, and she'd probably rolled over on it.

Determined to shake the flush from her face and to pretend that her ankles weren't bound together with duct tape, that her brain hadn't been abducted by aliens, Catherine forced herself to step forward and reach out to shake the neighboring rancher's hand. "It's nice to meet you, Ray. Eva said you'd be coming to dinner tonight. Please come in."

The handsome rancher's smile deepened, lighting his eyes, which were a vibrant shade of green.

As he released his grip on her hand, leaving her skin warm and tingling, he lifted a lazy index finger and peeled another sticker from her face.

Her lips parted as he showed her a little pink heart.

"You missed a couple of them," he said.

Huh? A couple of...what?

He removed a gold star from over her brow and a unicorn from her chin.

Catherine blinked back her surprise, as well as her embarrassment. Then she swiped her hand first over one cheek and then the other, discovering that either Sofia or Stephen had decorated her face while she'd slept.

Goodness. What else had the twins done to her while she'd been asleep? Surely they hadn't used their Magic Markers on her, too?

She hadn't felt the least bit self-conscious in years, but it all came rushing back at her now. She must look like a clown. What must the man be thinking?

Calling on her acting skills and her ability to ad-lib

on stage, she gave a little shrug, as if this sort of thing happened all the time. "Well, what do you know? The sticker fairies stopped by while I napped."

Ray tossed her a crooked grin, humor sparking in his eyes. "You've got to watch out for those fairies, especially on the Walker Ranch. There's no telling what they'll do next."

"I'm afraid he's right about that," Dan said as he entered the living room. "Our younger twins can be little rascals at times."

Before Catherine could respond, Dan greeted his friend with a handshake, then invited him to take a seat, suggesting that she do the same.

But there was no way Catherine wanted to remain in the living room looking like a ragamuffin, so she said, "I'd better help Eva in the kitchen."

"I was just in there," Dan said. "And she has everything under control."

Catherine didn't care where she went—to the kitchen, her bedroom or the barn. All she wanted to do was to disappear from the handsome rancher's sight until she could find a mirror before dinner.

"Well, since Eva doesn't need my help, I'll just go freshen up." She lobbed Ray Mendez her best, unaffected smile. "It was nice meeting you."

"The pleasure was mine."

The sound of the word *pleasure* on the lips of a man who not only resembled a Latin lover but sounded like one, too, was enough to knock her little Texas world off its axis.

And until she flew back to Manhattan, she'd do

whatever it took to keep her feet on solid ground in Brighton Valley.

One screwed-up world was more than she cared to handle.

Ray Mendez had no idea who Catherine Loza was, why she'd been napping this late in the afternoon or why she'd been included to have dinner at the Walkers' ranch. He watched her leave the room, turn down the hall and walk toward the bedrooms.

The minute she was out of hearing range, he turned to his neighbor and friend. "You're not starting in on me, too, are you?"

"*Starting in* on you? What do you mean?"

Ray crossed his arms and tensed. "Is this dinner supposed to be a setup?"

Dan looked a little confused by the question—or rather the accusation. "A *setup?* You mean, with you and *Catherine?* No, I wouldn't do that." Then he glanced toward the kitchen, as if realizing his pretty wife might have had a plan of her own.

But why wouldn't she? Every time Ray turned around, one of the women in town was trying to play matchmaker.

"Eva called and asked you to dinner because we hadn't seen you in a while," Dan said. "Why would you think we had anything else in mind?"

"Because ever since word got out that my divorce was final, the local matchmakers have come out of the woodwork, determined to find the perfect second wife for me. And the last thing I'm looking for right now is romance. I've got my hands full trying to run my ranch from a distance and finish out the term of the previous mayor."

"Has it been that bad?" Dan asked.

"You have no idea."

"For the record," Dan said, "Catherine is a great woman. She's beautiful, talented and has a heart of gold. But she's just visiting us. Her life is in New York, and yours is here. So it would be a waste of time to try my hand at matchmaking."

That was a relief. Thank God Ray's friends hadn't joined every marriage-minded woman in town—or her well-intentioned best friend, mother or neighbor.

He unfolded his arms and let down his guard.

As he did so, he glanced down the hall just as Catherine returned with her hair combed, those wild platinum curls controlled by a clip of some kind.

She'd changed into a pair of black jeans and a crisp, white blouse—nothing fancy. She'd also applied a light coat of pink lipstick and slipped on a pair of ballet flats.

For a moment, Ray wondered if she had romance on her mind. But the cynical thought passed as quickly as it had struck.

If Catherine had expected to meet someone special tonight, she wouldn't have opened the door with her hair a mess, stickers all over her face and no makeup whatsoever.

Although he had to admit, she'd looked pretty darn cute standing at the door, blue eyes wide, lips parted....

As Catherine crossed through the living room on her way to the kitchen, she gave him a passing smile.

And when she was again out of hearing range, Ray turned back to Dan. "Where'd you meet her?"

"She used to be Jenny's roommate."

Dan's sister, Jenny Walker, had left Brighton Valley after graduating from high school. She'd gone to college in the Midwest, majored in music or dance and moved to New York, where she'd done some singing and acting off-Broadway.

About eight or nine years ago, Jenny gave birth to twins, although she died when Kevin and Kaylee were in kindergarten. Dan and Eva adopted the kids and were now raising them, as well as their own younger set of twins.

"Catherine has come out a time or two to visit," Dan added, "but she never stayed long. She's an actress and a dancer, so she usually has a Broadway show of some kind going on."

"Is that what she's doing here now? Visiting the kids?"

"Actually, this time I'm not sure how long she'll be with us. She broke up with some hot-shot producer back in New York and wanted to get away for a while. I don't know all of the details, but it really doesn't matter. She stepped up to the plate and helped me and the kids out when we really needed her, so I'm happy to return the favor now."

Ray raked his hand through his hair. "I'm sorry for jumping to conclusions. I should have known you wouldn't have invited me to come over with more than dinner on your mind."

Dan studied him for a moment. "Is the matchmaking really that bad?"

He chuffed. "I can't make it through a single day without someone trying to set me up with a single daughter, niece or neighbor. And that's not counting the unmarried ladies who approach me on their own behalf." Ray grumbled under his breath, wishing he'd stayed out of politics and had remained on his ranch full-time.

"Well, I guess that's to be expected." A grin tugged at one side of Dan's lips, and his eyes lit up with mirth. "You're not a bad-looking fellow. And you've got a little cash put away. I guess that makes you an eligible bachelor in anyone's book."

"Very funny." Ray had never been full of himself, but most women considered him to be the tall, dark and handsome type. He also had a head for business, which had allowed him to parlay a couple of inheritances into millions. As a result, he had more money and property than he could shake a stick at, something that made every unattached female between the ages of 18 and 40 seem to think he was a prime catch.

He could always give them the cold shoulder, but his mother had taught him to be polite and courteous—a habit he found hard to shake. Besides, he didn't know how to keep the women at arm's distance without alienating half the voters in town.

"To top it off," Dan added, "you being the mayor gives you a little more status than just being a run-of-the-mill Texas rancher, which the ladies undoubtedly find even more appealing."

Ray sighed. "That's the problem. I'm not looking for romance. And if the time ever comes that I'm interested again, I'm perfectly capable of finding a woman without help."

Dan, who'd been biting back a full-on smile, let it go and chuckled. "There's got to be a lot of guys who'd be happy to trade places with you."

"Maybe, but only for a couple of days. Then they'd get fed up, too. This has been going on since...well, since word got out that my divorce was final. And now I can hardly get any work done—in town or on the ranch."

"Why *not* date someone, just so word will spread that you're already taken?"

Ray shook his head. "No, I'm not going to do that. After the marriage I had, I'm steering clear of women in general. But even if I wanted to ask someone out, I don't have the time to add anything else to my calendar. As it is, I've been spending the bulk of my day driving back and forth to the ranch, making sure Mark and Darren have everything under control, then zipping back to town for one meeting or another."

"I don't blame you for not wanting to jump back into another relationship, especially after the hell Heather put you through over the past two years."

Dan had that right. Ray's ex-wife had not only cheated on him, she'd turned out to be a heartless gold digger. And after the long legal battle she'd waged, Ray wasn't about to make a mistake like that again.

"You know," Dan said, "it might not be a bad idea to spread the rumor that you're already taken. Maybe that way, the matchmaking mamas and their starry-eyed daughters will give you a break and let you get some work done."

"That's an idea, but as simple and easy as it sounds, I'm afraid it won't work."

"Why not?"

"Because I'd keep showing up alone at all the various community events I'm required to attend, and people will begin to realize the woman is only a myth. And then I'll be right back where I started. I'm afraid I'd need the real thing, and that would defeat the purpose of creating a fictitious woman."

"Too bad you can't rent an escort," Dan said.

"Yeah, right."

At that moment, Catherine reentered the living room and called Dan's name. "Eva said to tell you that dinner's ready. She's already called Hank, and he's heading over here now."

"Thanks," Dan said. "We'll be right there."

As Catherine returned to the kitchen, Ray watched the sway of her denim-clad hips. It was hard to imagine her as a woman who was at home on the stage, especially since she had a wholesome, girl-next-door appeal. But then again, she *was* an actress....

Suddenly, an idea began to form.

"How long does Catherine plan to be in town?" he asked.

"I'm not sure. Why?"

"Do you think she'd want a job?"

"Probably. Just this morning she mentioned that she'd like to find something part-time and temporary. Why?"

"Because I want to hire her, if she's interested."

"What did you have in mind? Something clerical?"

"No, it would be an acting job."

Dan looked confused. "I'm not following you."

A slow smile stretched across Ray's face. "I'd like to hire Catherine to be my fiancée."

After dinner and dessert had been served, Dan's uncle thanked Eva for another wonderful meal, then headed back to his place so he could watch his favorite TV show.

Eva sent the older twins to get ready for bed, then she and Dan gathered up the preschoolers and told them it was bath time, leaving Catherine and Ray in the dining room.

"Can I get you another cup of coffee?" Catherine asked.

"That sounds good. Thanks."

Minutes later she returned with the carafe and filled his cup, then her own.

"Dan told me that you might be interested in some part-time work," Ray said.

Catherine had no idea how long she'd be in Brighton Valley, but it would probably be at least a month. So she'd thought about trying to earn a little cash while she was here.

Of course, if truth be told, she didn't have many skills that would come in handy in a place like Brighton Valley.

"I'm interested," she said, lifting her coffee cup and taking a sip. "As long as it was only temporary. Do you know of a position that's open?"

"Yes, I do. And it's probably right up your alley."

Catherine couldn't imagine what it might be. She was just about to ask for more details when she realized that Ray had zeroed in on her again, as if mesmerized or intrigued by her.

If she were in Manhattan, dressed to the nines, she might have taken his interest as a compliment. As it was, she didn't know what to think.

"What kind of job is it?" she asked.

"It's a little unorthodox," he admitted, "but it's only part-time, and the money's good."

"Who would I be working for? And what would I be doing?"

"You'd be working for me. I need an actress, and you'd be perfect for the part."

"I don't understand." Catherine lifted her cup and took another sip.

"I need a fiancée," Ray said.

Catherine choked on her coffee. "*Excuse* me?"

"I want people in town to think that I'm in a committed relationship. And Dan thinks you have the acting skills to pull it off."

"Why in the world would a man like you need to hire a girlfriend?" Once the words were off her tongue, she wanted to take them back. "I'm sorry," she said. "I'm not sure I'm following you."

"Okay, let me explain. I need a temporary escort to attend various community functions with me, and it would be best if people had the idea that we were serious about each other."

Did he think that was an explanation? He'd merely reworded the job description.

"There are a lot of single women in town who've been making my life difficult," he added. "And for some reason, they seem to think I'm actively looking for another wife."

"But you're *not?*"

"No. At least, not for the foreseeable future. My divorce became final a month ago, although my ex-wife moved out nearly two years ago. So I'm not in any hurry to jump into another relationship. I've tried to explain that to people, but apparently they don't believe me."

"Maybe you should be more direct."

"I thought I was. And I'd rather not alienate or anger any of my constituents."

Constituents? Oh, yes. Eva had mentioned he was also the mayor of Brighton Valley. So that meant he was dealing with small-town politics.

Either way Catherine thought the whole idea was a little weird—if not a bit laughable. But then again, she could use the work—and she *was* an actress.

"How long do you need my help?" she asked.

"Until my interim position as mayor is over—or for as long as you're in town. Whichever comes first."

He seemed to have it all planned out.

"I'll pay you a thousand dollars a week," he added.

Catherine was still trying to wrap her mind around his job offer, which was crazy. But the money he would pay spoke louder than the craziness, and against her better judgment, she found herself leaning toward an agreement.

"What would your fiancée have to do?" she asked.

Ray sketched an appreciative gaze over her that sent her senses reeling and had her wondering just how far he'd want her to go in playing the part.

"I have to attend a lot of events and fundraisers, so it would be nice to have you go with me whenever possible. I even have a ring for you to wear on your left hand, which you can return when the job is over."

He was including the props?

This was wild. Pretending to be engaged to Ray Mendez was probably the craziest job offer she'd ever had, but she supposed it really didn't matter. If he was willing to pay for her acting skills, then why not go along with it?

"All right," she finally said. "You've got yourself a deal. When do I start?"

"Why don't you meet me for lunch at Caroline's tomorrow? A lot of the locals will be there, so it'll be a good way to send out the message that I'm already taken."

"And then…?"

"I don't know." He stroked his square-cut jaw. "Maybe I could greet you with a kiss, then we'll play it by ear. Hopefully, the rumor mill will kick into gear right away."

"What if it doesn't?"

He gave a half shrug. "I guess we'll have to take things day by day."

"So you just want me to have lunch with you tomorrow?"

"Actually, later that evening, I also have a charity event to attend at the Brighton Valley Medical Center. It's a benefit for the new neonatal intensive care unit, and it would probably be a good idea if we walked in together, holding hands. Maybe, if you looked at me a little starry-eyed, people would get the message."

"You want me to look at you *starry-eyed?*"

"Hell, I don't know how to explain it. You're a woman—and an actress. Just do whatever you'd do if we were actually engaged or at least committed to each other. I want people to think we're a real couple."

"Okay. I can do that. But what's the dress code tomorrow night?"

"I'll be wearing a sport jacket."

She bit down on her bottom lip, then glanced down at the simple blouse and black jeans she was wearing now. If truth be told, it was the fanciest outfit she'd brought with her.

"What's the matter?" he asked.

"If we were in New York, it wouldn't be a problem for me to find the right thing to wear. But I'm afraid I didn't plan to do anything other than kick back on the ranch and play with the kids while I'm here, so I only packed casual outfits."

"That's not a problem." He scooted back his chair and reached into the pocket of his jeans. He pulled out a money clip with a wad of bills, peeled off three hundred dollars and handed it to her. "After lunch tomorrow you can walk down the street to The Boutique. It's a shop located a few doors down from the diner."

Catherine couldn't imagine what type of clothing she'd find in Brighton Valley, but then again, she'd chosen to come to Texas because it was light-years from Manhattan and her memories there. She supposed she would have to adjust her tastes to the styles small-town women found appealing—or at least affordable.

She stole another glance at the handsome rancher

seated across the table from her to find that he was studying her, too. Sexual awareness fluttered through her like a swarm of lovesick butterflies.

But that shouldn't surprise her. Ray Mendez was a handsome man. No wonder every woman in town was after him.

Of course, he was paying her to keep the other women at bay.

It would be an easy job, she decided—and one she might actually enjoy. Her biggest Broadway role had been the mistress of a 1920s Chicago mobster. The actor who'd played her lover had been twenty years older than she and about forty pounds overweight. His ruddy appearance had suited the character he'd played, although it had taken some real skills on her part to pretend she was sexually attracted to him.

Ray Mendez was going to make a much better costar, though—especially if her role was going to require a few starry-eyed gazes, some hand-holding and maybe a kiss or two.

For the first time since leaving Manhattan, she was actually looking forward to getting on stage again.

Chapter Two

At a few minutes before noon, Ray stood in front of Caroline's Diner, waiting for his hired fiancée to arrive. The plan had been for Catherine to borrow Eva's minivan, then to meet him in town.

To his surprise, he was actually looking forward to seeing her again—and not just because she was the solution to one of his many problems.

Even when she'd been wearing sweatpants and an oversize T-shirt, the tall, leggy blonde with bed-head curls had been a lovely sight. Her blue-green eyes—almost a turquoise shade, really—and an expressive smile only added to the overall effect.

Of course, those little heart and flower stickers that the younger Walker twins had stuck on her face while she'd slept had been an interesting touch.

When Ray had pointed them out, she'd made a joke of it without missing a beat. And that meant she would probably be able to handle anything the townspeople might throw at her. If anyone quizzed her about their past or their plans for the future, she'd be quick on her feet.

They hadn't talked much after dinner last night, since Dan and Eva had returned to the table once they'd gotten the kids in bed. But they'd managed to concoct a believable past for their imaginary romance.

Fortunately, she wasn't a well-known Broadway actress, so they'd agreed to tell people they'd met in Houston six months ago and that they'd been dating ever since.

The day Ray's divorce had been final—after two long years in legal limbo—he'd proposed over a glass of champagne during a candlelit dinner in the city. She'd accepted, although they'd decided not to make an official announcement of their engagement until she could take some vacation time and come to Brighton Valley.

So now here he was, standing outside Caroline's Diner, ready to reveal their phony engagement to the locals who'd already begun to file into the small restaurant and fill the tables.

Ray glanced at his wristwatch again, knowing that he'd arrived a few minutes early and realizing that Catherine really wasn't late. Rather, he was a little nervous. Could they pull it off?

"Hello, Mayor," a woman called out in a chipper voice.

Ray glanced up to see Melanie Robertson approaching the diner wearing a smile.

Aw, man. This was just the kind of thing he'd been trying to avoid. Where was his "fiancée" when he needed her?

"Are you waiting for someone?" Melanie asked. "Or would you like to join Carla Guerrero and me for lunch?"

"Thanks for the offer, but I am meeting someone."

"Is it business or pleasure?" she asked, her lashes fluttering in a flirtatious manner.

"It's definitely pleasure." Out of the corner of his eye he spotted Catherine walking down the street. At least, that tall, blonde stranger striding toward him appeared to be the woman he'd met last night.

She'd told him that she hadn't brought anything fancy to Texas, but…hot damn. She hadn't needed a shopping trip for their lunch today. A pair of tight jeans, a little makeup and a dab of lipstick had made a stunning transformation from attractive girl next door to dazzling.

"Hi, honey." Catherine burst into a smile as she reached him. "I'm sorry I'm late."

Then she leaned forward and brushed her lips across his, giving him a brief hint of peppermint breath mints.

Her fragrance—something light and exotic—snaked around him, squeezing the air out of his lungs and making it nearly impossible to speak.

Then she turned to Melanie, offered a confident, bright-eyed smile and reached out her hand in greeting. "Hi, I'm Catherine Loza."

The same pesky cat that seemed to have gotten Ray's tongue appeared to have captured Melanie's, as well. He could understand her surprised reaction to Catherine's arrival and greeting, but not his own. Not when he'd been the one to set up the whole fake fiancée thing in the first place.

So why had Catherine's performance set *him* off balance?

Because she was so damn good at what she was doing, he supposed.

Shaking off the real effects of the pretend kiss, he introduced the women, adding, "Melanie's family owns the ice cream shop down the street."

"It's nice to meet you," Catherine said.

Melanie, whose eyes kept bouncing from Ray to his "date" and back again, said, "Same here. I…uh…" She nodded toward the entrance of Caroline's Diner. "I came to have lunch with a coworker, so I guess I'll see you two inside." Then she reached for the door and let herself in.

Well, what do you know? Catherine had been on the job only a minute or two, and the ploy was already working like a charm.

When they were alone, she asked, "So how did I do?"

"You were great." In fact, she was better than great. She both looked and acted the part of a loving fiancée, and even Ray found himself believing the romantic story they'd concocted was true.

"Now what?" she asked. "Did you want to go inside?"

"Yes, but I've got something to give you first.

Come with me." Ray led her to the street corner, then turned to the left. When they reached the alley, he made a second left.

Once they were out of plain sight, he reached into the lapel pocket of his leather jacket and removed a small, velvet-covered box. Then he lifted the lid and revealed an engagement ring.

"Will this work?" he asked.

Catherine's breath caught as she peered at what appeared to be an antique, which had been cleaned and polished. The diamond, while fairly small, glistened in the sunlight.

"It was my grandmother's," he said.

"It's beautiful." She doubted the ring was costly, but she imagined that the sentimental value was priceless. "I've never had an heirloom, so I'll take good care of it."

Then she removed the ring from the box and slipped it on the ring finger of her left hand, surprised that it actually fit.

For a moment, she wondered about the woman who'd worn it before her, about the relationship she'd had with her husband—and with her grandson. She suspected they'd been close.

When she looked at Ray, when their eyes met and their gazes locked, she asked, "What was her name?"

The question seemed to sideswipe him. *"Who?"*

"Your grandmother."

He paused, as if the reminder had surprised him as much as the question had, then said, "Her name was Elena."

Catherine lifted her hand and studied the setting

a bit longer. It was an old-fashioned piece of jewelry, yet it had been polished to a pretty shine.

When she looked up again, he was watching her intently.

"What's the matter?" she asked.

He didn't respond right away, and when she thought that he might not, he said, "I know that ring isn't anything most people would consider impressive, but it meant a lot to my grandmother."

Catherine's mother had worn a single gold band, although she wasn't sure it had meant much to her. And when she'd passed away, the family had buried her with it still on her finger. As far as Catherine knew, not one of her siblings had mentioned wanting to inherit it.

But Ray's ring was different—special.

"It's actually an honor to wear this." She studied the setting a moment longer, then turned to Ray, whose gaze nearly set her heart on end.

So she repeated what she'd told him before, "I'll take good care of it while it's in my possession."

"Thanks. I'm glad you can appreciate the sentiment attached to it. Not all women can."

He'd mentioned being recently divorced, so she couldn't help wondering if he was talking about his ex-wife.

Had she worn it? Had she given it back to him when they'd split?

Not that it mattered, she supposed.

"So," he said, "are you ready to have lunch now?"

When she nodded, he took her hand and led her back to the diner, where they would begin their performance. They were a team, she supposed. Costars in a sense.

They also had something else in common—hearts on the mend.

Ray opened the glass door, allowing Catherine to enter first. While waiting for him to choose a table, she scanned the quaint interior of the small-town eatery, with its white café-style curtains on the front windows, as well as the yellow walls that were adorned by a trellis of daisies on the wallpaper border.

To the right of an old-fashioned cash register stood a refrigerated display case filled with pies and cakes—each one clearly homemade.

She glanced at a blackboard that advertised a full meal for only $7.99.

In bright yellow chalk, someone had written, *What the Sheriff Ate,* followed by, *Chicken-Fried Steak, Buttered Green Beans, Mashed Potatoes, Country Gravy and Apple Pie.*

The advertised special sounded delicious, but she'd have to watch what she ate today. When she'd gotten dressed back at the ranch, she'd struggled to zip her jeans and found them so snug in the waist that she'd been tempted to leave the top button undone or to wear something else.

If she didn't start cutting out all the fat and the carbs she'd been consuming since arriving in Brighton Valley, she was going to return to New York twenty pounds heavier. And where would that leave her when it came time to audition for her next part?

Of course, after that stunt Erik Carmichael had

pulled, she'd be lucky if other producers didn't black-ball her by association alone.

How could she have been so gullible, so blind? The one person she'd trusted completely had pulled the cashmere over her eyes. And while she feared that she'd been hard-pressed to trust another man again, it was her own gullibility that frightened her the most.

As Ray placed his hand on her lower back, claiming her in an intimate way, she shook off the bad memories and focused on the here and now.

"There's a place for us to sit." With his hand still warming her back, he ushered her to a table for two in the center of the restaurant, then pulled out her chair.

It was the perfect spot, she supposed. Everyone in the diner would see them together, which was what Ray had planned—and what he was paying for. So as soon as he'd taken the seat across from hers, she leaned forward, placed her hand over the top of his and put on her happiest smile. "I've missed you, Ray. It's so good to be together again."

His lips quirked into a crooked grin, and his green eyes sparked. "It's been rough, hasn't it?"

When she nodded, he tilted his hand to the side, wrapped his fingers around hers and gave them a gentle, affectionate squeeze. "I'm glad to have you with me for a change."

Before Catherine could manage a response, a salt-and-pepper-haired waitress stopped by their table and smiled. "Hello, Mayor. Can I get you and your friend something to drink?"

"You sure can, Margie. I'd like a glass of iced tea."

Ray gave Catherine's hand another little squeeze. "What would you like, honey?"

"Water will be fine."

At the term of endearment, Margie's head tilted to the side. Then her gaze zeroed in on their clasped hands. Instead of heading for the kitchen, she paused, her eyes widening and her lips parting.

"We'll need a few minutes to look over the menu," Ray told the stunned waitress.

Margie lingered a moment, as if she'd lost track of what she was doing. Then she addressed Catherine. "I haven't seen you in town before. Are you new or just passing through?"

Catherine offered her a friendly smile. "I'm visiting for the next couple of weeks, but I'm not really passing through. I plan to move here before the end of summer."

"Well, now. Isn't that nice." Margie shifted her weight to one hip, clearly intrigued by Catherine. "Where are you staying?"

"With *me*," Ray said. "You're the first one outside the Walker family to meet my fiancée, Margie."

"Well, now. Imagine that." The waitress beamed, her cheeks growing rosy. "What a nice surprise. Of course, there's going to be a lot of heartbroken young women in town when they learn that our handsome young mayor is…already taken."

"I doubt that anyone will shed a tear over that," Ray said, turning to Catherine and giving her a wink. "But I'm definitely taken. And I was from the very first moment I laid eyes on her in Houston."

Catherine reached for the menu with her left hand,

taking care to flash the diamond on her finger. Then she stole a peek at Margie to see if the older woman had noticed—and she had.

When the waitress finally left the table, Ray said, "Margie is a great gal, but she's a real talker. By nightfall, the news of our engagement will be all over town."

As Catherine scanned the diner, which had filled with the lunch crowd, she realized that Margie might not have to say much at all, since everyone else seemed to be focusing their attention on her and coming to their own conclusions.

"So what are you going to have?" she asked as she opened the menu and tried to get back into character.

"If I hadn't already eaten a good breakfast at the Rotary Club meeting this morning, I'd have the daily special. But Caroline's helpings are usually more than filling, so I'll probably get a sandwich instead."

Moments later, Margie returned with her pad and pencil, ready to take their orders. "So what'll you have?"

"I'd like the cottage cheese and fruit," Catherine said.

Ray asked for a BLT with fries.

After jotting down their requests, Margie remained at the table, her eyes on Catherine. "So what do you think of Brighton Valley so far?"

"It's a lovely town. I'm going to like living here."

"I'm sure you will." Margie smiled wistfully. "My husband and I came here to visit his sister one summer, and we were so impressed with the people and the small-town atmosphere that we went back to Austin, sold our house and moved out here for good. In fact, it was the single best thing we ever did for our family. Brighton Valley has got to be the greatest place in the world to raise kids."

"That's what I've been telling her," Ray said. "So I'm glad you're backing me up."

"Well, let me be the first to congratulate you on your engagement," Margie said, "and to welcome you to the best little town in all of Texas."

"Thank you."

Margie nodded toward the kitchen. "Well, it was nice meeting you, but I'd better turn in your orders before you die of hunger."

When the waitress left them alone again, Ray reached into his pocket, pulled out a single key, as well as a business card, and handed it to Catherine. "This will get you into the apartment I keep in town, which is just down the street. I'll point it out to you later."

She placed the key into the pocket on the inside of her purse, then fingered the card with his contact information at both the Broken M Ranch and City Hall.

"After you go shopping at The Boutique," he added, "you can hang out and wait for me at my place. I should be home by five or five-thirty."

"All right. I'll be dressed and ready to go by the time you get there."

"Good. I've got some snacks in the pantry and drinks in the fridge. But if there's anything else you need, give me a call and I'll pick it up for you."

Anything she needed?

For the hospital benefit? Or was he talking about the duration of her acting gig?

She recalled the day Erik Carmichael had given her the key to his place, pretty much telling her the same thing, so she wasn't sure.

"Did you bring an overnight bag?" he asked.

No, only her makeup pouch. He hadn't said anything about spending the night.

Where are you staying? Margie had asked Ray just moments ago. And without batting an eye, he'd said, *With me.*

Was he expecting Catherine to actually move into his apartment while they pretended to be lovers? He hadn't mentioned anything about that when they'd discussed the job and his expectations last night.

"We'll probably be out late this evening," he added, then he bent forward and lowered his voice to a whisper. "It'll be easier that way."

She supposed it would be. And if they wanted everyone in town to assume they were lovers, staying together would make the whole idea a lot more believable.

They could, she supposed, talk about the sleeping arrangements later, but she assumed that she'd be using the sofa.

Of course, she wasn't sure what he had in mind, but she'd have to deal with that when the time came. Right now, she had a job to do.

She had to convince everyone in town that she was Ray Mendez's fiancée.

After Ray had paid the bill and left Margie a generous tip, he opened the door for Catherine and waited for her to exit. Once he'd followed her outside, they would be the talk of the diner, and that was just what he'd wanted.

Catherine had done all he'd asked of her. She'd looked at him a little starry-eyed, and she'd also used her hands when she'd talked, which had shown off the diamond his grandfather had placed upon his grandmother's finger more than seventy-five years ago.

She'd seemed to be genuinely impressed by the ring, although he supposed that could have been part of the act. But something told him that wasn't the case, which was more than a little surprising.

Before offering the ring to Heather, he'd had it cleaned and polished. But she'd turned up her nose at wearing something that wasn't brand-new and expensive. So, like a fool, he'd gone into Houston and purchased her a two-carat diamond, which she'd taken with her when she'd told him she wanted a divorce and moved out of the ranch house.

He supposed he'd have to be thankful for Heather's greed in that respect. Otherwise, he would have lost his grandmother's ring completely—or paid through the nose to get it back, since Heather had known how much it had meant to him. And if she'd had one more thing to hold over him, they might still be in the midst of divorce negotiations.

On the other hand, Catherine seemed to have a lot more respect for the family heirloom. When she'd studied the diamond in the sunlight, she'd even asked his grandmother's name, although Ray had been so caught up in the memory of Heather scrunching up her face at the ring that Catherine's question had completely sideswiped him.

Now, as they stood outside the diner, in the mottled shade of one of the many elm trees that lined Main Street, Ray pointed to his right. "The Boutique is located right next to the ice cream shop. And several doors down, you'll see the drugstore. There's a little red door to the left of it, which is the stairway that leads to my apartment."

"Thanks. After I buy the dress, I'll probably do some window shopping while I'm here. If anyone asks me who I am, I'll tell them I'm your fiancée. And that I'm staying with you."

"That's a good idea." He probably ought to start the walk back to City Hall, but for some reason, he couldn't quite tear himself away.

Outside, even in the dappled sunlight, the platinum strands of her hair glistened like white gold. And when she looked at him like that, smiling as though they were both involved in some kind of romantic secret, he noticed the green flecks in her irises that made her eyes appear to be a turquoise shade. It was an amazing color.

And she was an amazing…*actress*.

In fact, she was so good at what she did that he'd have to be careful not to confuse what was real and what wasn't.

"Thanks for helping me out," he said.

"You're welcome." She didn't budge either, which meant she was waiting for him to make the first move. But there were people seated near the windows of Caroline's Diner, people who were watching the two phony lovers through the glass.

"Well, I'd better go," he said. "I've got to get back

to City Hall before it gets much later. Do you have enough money to cover the dress and any incidentals you might need?"

She patted the side of her purse. "I sure do. And it's plenty. I'll probably have change to give you this evening when you get home."

Change? Now, that was a surprise. Even when they'd only been dating, Heather would have spent the entire wad and then some. And once he'd slipped a ring on her finger…well, things had just gone from bad to worse.

He was just about to say goodbye and send Catherine on her way when she eased forward, rose on tiptoe and lifted her lips to kiss him goodbye.

Of course.

Great idea.

There was an audience present, and they were two people in love. A goodbye kiss was definitely in order.

Ray stepped in and lowered his mouth to hers, but as their lips met, he found himself wrapping his arms around her and pulling her close, savoring the feel of her in his arms, the scent of her shampoo, the taste of her….

Oh, wow.

As he slipped into fiancé mode, the kiss seemed to take on a life of its own, deepening—although not in a sexual or inappropriate public display. In fact, to anyone who might be peering at them from inside the diner, their parting kiss would appear to be sweet and affectionate.

Yet on the inside of Ray, where no one else was privy, it caused his gut to clench and his blood to stir.

She placed her hand—the one that bore his grandmother's ring—on his face and smiled adoringly. As she slowly dropped her left hand, her fingers trailed down his cheek, sending ripples of heat radiating to his jaw and taunting him with sexual awareness.

Damn she was good. She even had *him* thinking there was something going on between them. No wonder Hollywood actors and actresses were constantly switching partners.

He'd best keep that fact in mind. The last thing in the world he needed to do was to get caught up in the act and to confuse fantasy with reality.

Chapter Three

When Ray entered his apartment at a quarter to five, he found Catherine seated on the sofa, watching television.

"You're home early," she said, reaching for the remote. After turning off the power, she stood to greet him.

But just the sight of the tall, shapely blonde wearing a classic black dress and heels made him freeze in his tracks.

"What do you think?" She turned around, showing him the new outfit she'd chosen.

"It's amazing," he said. And he wasn't just talking about the dress. Her transformation from actress to cover model had nearly thrown him for a loop.

Each time he saw Catherine, she morphed into a woman who was even more beautiful than the last.

Is that what dating an actress would be like? Having a different woman each time they went out?

If so, the part of him that enjoyed an occasional male fantasy sat up and took notice.

"I even found a pair of heels and an evening bag," she said, striding for the lamp table to show him a small beaded purse.

"You found all of that at The Boutique?" He'd expected her to complain about the out-of-date inventory at Brighton Valley's only ladies dress shop. Heather, who wasn't even from a place as style conscious as New York, certainly had.

"No," Catherine said, "I had to go to Zapatos, the shoe store across the street, for the heels and bag. What do you think? Will this do?"

Would it *do?*

"Absolutely." She looked like a million bucks, which had him thinking he'd better reach for his wallet. "I couldn't have given you enough money to pay for all of that."

"Oh, yes, you did." She smiled, lighting those blue-green eyes and revealing two of the prettiest dimples he'd ever seen. "I even have a few dollars change for you."

Again, the compulsion to compare her to his ex-wife struck him hard, but he shook it off. Heather was long gone—thank goodness. And now, thanks to Catherine, Ray wouldn't need to weed out the gold diggers from the dating pool until he was ready to.

"I'll take a quick shower," he said. "Just give me a couple of minutes."

After snatching his clothes from the bedroom, he

headed for the bathroom. Then, once inside, he turned on the spigot and waited for the water to heat.

Surprisingly, he was actually looking forward to attending the hospital benefit tonight, especially since he would walk in with Catherine on his arm. A man could get used to looking at a woman like her—and talking to her, too.

Of course, he was paying her to be pleasant and agreeable. If they'd met on different terms, it might be another story altogether.

He had to admit that he'd gone out on a limb by hiring a fake fiancée, but after all he'd been through with Heather, after all their divorce had cost him, he wasn't ready to date again. And even when he was ready to give it another go, he didn't think he'd ever want to get married again.

What a nightmare his marriage had turned out to be.

Of course, if he wanted to have a child, he'd have to reconsider. After all, as the only son of an only son, Ray had no one to leave his ranch and holdings to unless he had an heir. But he was still young—thirty-six on his next birthday—so he had plenty of time to think about having children.

He reached into the shower stall and felt the water growing warm, so he peeled off his clothes and stepped under the steady stream of water. As he reached for the bar of soap, he found Catherine's lavender-colored razor resting next to it, along with her yellow bath gel.

It was weird to see feminine toiletries in his bathroom again. He'd been living without a woman under his roof for nearly two years, so he'd gotten used to having the place to himself.

Still, he reached for the plastic bottle, popped open the lid and took a whiff of Catherine's soap. The exotic floral fragrance reminded him of her.

Again he realized that he could get used to coming home to a beautiful blonde like Catherine, to having her ask how his day went, to stepping into her embrace and breathing in her scent. But the Catherine who'd spent the lunch hour with him earlier today wasn't real.

He'd employed her to be the perfect fiancée, and she was merely doing her job.

Even if he got caught up in the act, if he let down his guard, believing Catherine was different and allowing himself to see her in a romantic light, he'd be making another big mistake.

After all, he'd made up his mind to steer clear of big-city women from here on out—and cities didn't get much bigger than Manhattan.

Besides, he now realized that he needed someone with both of her feet firmly planted on Brighton Valley soil.

And Catherine was only passing through.

Ray snatched one of the brown fluffy towels from the rack on the wall and dried off. After shaving and splashing on a bit of cologne, he put on his clothes—black slacks and a white dress shirt, which he left open at the collar.

After he'd combed his hair, he removed his black, Western-cut jacket from the hanger and slipped it on.

Then he returned to the living room where Catherine waited for him.

She wasn't watching television this time. She was standing near the window, looking out onto Main Street. She turned when she heard his footsteps, gave him a once-over and smiled. "You look great."

He didn't know about that, but he figured people were going to think that they'd planned coordinating outfits.

"Thanks," he said. "So do you. You're going to knock the socks off every man at the benefit—married or not."

"Well, you're no slouch, Mayor. Especially when you get all dressed up. So maybe I ought to worry about running into a few jealous women tonight." A slow smile stretched across her face. "I might have to charge hazard pay."

He chuckled. "There might be a few who'll be sorry to learn I'm taken, but they'll be polite about it." He nodded toward the bedroom door. "I need to get my boots. I'll be right back."

Minutes later, he returned to the living room, ready to go.

"So tell me," Catherine said, as she reached for her small, beaded evening bag. "What made you decide to run for mayor of Brighton Valley?"

"I didn't actually run for mayor. Six months ago, after a couple of beers down at the Stagecoach Inn, I had a weak moment and agreed to run for a vacant city council seat. I'd never really wanted to get involved in politics, so I almost backed out the next day.

But then I realized I might be able to make a difference in the community, so I went through with it."

"Apparently the citizens of Brighton Valley agreed with you."

"I guess you're right, because I won hands down. Then, a few weeks ago, Jim Cornwall, the elected mayor, was trimming a tree in his backyard and fell off the ladder. He suffered a skull fracture, as well as several other serious injuries. He'll be laid up for some time, so I was asked to fill the position until he returns."

"That's quite the compliment," she said.

"You're right, which is why I reluctantly agreed. Trouble was, I had enough on my plate already, with a land deal I'm in the midst of negotiating and a new horse-breeding operation that's just getting under way."

Then, on top of that, his life had been further complicated by all the single women coming out of the woodwork, now that he was single again. And if there was anything he didn't need in his life right now, it was more complications—especially of the female variety.

"Something tells me you'll be able to handle it."

She was right, of course. Ray Mendez was no quitter. He was also an idea man who could think himself out of most any dilemma.

So here he was, preparing to go to a charity event at the Brighton Valley Medical Center with a hired fiancée, albeit a lovely woman who was sure to make a splash when they walked into the hospital side by side.

Ray had never been one to want center stage, yet

he didn't really mind it tonight, since he knew he'd be in good hands with an accomplished actress. So, with their employment agreement binding them, they were about to make their evening debut.

Now, as he opened the door of his apartment, the curtain was going up and the show was on. He probably ought to have a little stage fright, but he wasn't the least bit apprehensive.

Catherine, as he'd found out at their matinee performance earlier today, just outside Caroline's Diner, was one heck of an actress. All he had to do was to follow her lead.

In fact, he was looking forward to being with her tonight, to watching their act unfold.

When it was over, they'd head back to his place. He wasn't sure what would happen after that. They'd have a debriefing, he supposed. And maybe they'd kick back and watch a little TV.

He really hadn't given the rest of the evening any thought. Yet something told him he should have. He was finding his hired fiancée a little too attractive to just let the chips fall where they might.

As Catherine and Ray entered the hospital pavilion, which had been decorated with blinking white lights, black tablecloths and vases of red roses, she instinctively reached for his hand.

She wished she could say it had been part of the act, but the truth was, she was having a bit of stage fright—as unusual as that was.

He wrapped his fingers around hers and gave them a conspiratorial squeeze. "Good idea."

She wished she could have taken full credit for the hand-holding, but she'd done it without any forethought.

During the ten-minute drive from his downtown apartment to the medical center, she'd been so engrossed by the tall, dark and handsome man across the seat from her, so mesmerized by his sexy Texas drawl, that she couldn't help thinking of this evening as a date, rather than a job. So when they'd entered the pavilion and she'd spotted a sea of strangers, she'd reached for a friend.

At least, that's the way it had felt at the time.

But he was right; slipping her hand into his had been the perfect move—under the circumstances.

So what if his warm grip was actually comforting and she found herself feeling energized by the connection, strengthened by it.

Ray led her toward a petite Latina who was greeting an older man dressed in a gray suit and bold tie.

"I want to introduce you to Dr. Ramirez," he said upon their approach. "She's one of the major players trying to fund a neonatal intensive care unit at Brighton Valley Medical Center."

The attractive doctor who, even in high heels, didn't appear to be much taller than five foot two, was stylishly dressed in turquoise and black.

"Selena," Ray said, "I'd like you to meet my fiancée, Catherine Loza."

The doctor brightened, and as she reached out in greeting, Catherine released her hold on Ray long enough to give the woman a polite shake.

"I didn't realize Ray was engaged," Selena Ramirez said, "but it's no surprise. He's a great guy."

"I couldn't agree more." Catherine wondered if Selena had been one of the single women in town who'd been after Ray, although she certainly wasn't giving off those kinds of vibes now.

Even Melanie Robertson, the woman she'd met in front of the diner, had seemed a little disappointed—and maybe even envious—when she'd gotten the message that the handsome, single mayor was now taken.

"Selena is an obstetrician," Ray added. "She's been actively working with the city council to support the efforts to build the NICU."

"As it is," Selena explained, "our smallest preemies have to be airlifted to Houston. And I'd like to provide our mothers with the assurance that their babies are getting the best care available here at the medical center."

Ray nodded in agreement. "That reality really hit home for all of us when one of the councilmen's granddaughter was born. She had some serious problems at birth and had to be transported to the nearest neonatal unit. That's when we agreed to open our wallets and do whatever we could to help."

"That must have been a scary time for the councilman's family," Catherine said.

"It was." Selena's face grew solemn. "And sadly, their baby didn't make it."

Just hearing of a new mother's loss tore at Catherine's heart. She loved children and had hoped to have one or two of her own someday, but she'd had so many female problems in the past, including cysts on one of her ovaries and surgery to remove it, that the doctors had told her years ago that she wasn't likely to conceive. So her chances of having a baby of her own were slim to none.

She'd been more than a little disappointed upon learning the news, but she'd come to grips with it.

"I'd be happy to lend my support," Catherine said. "When Jennifer Walker's twins were born, they were several weeks early. But thanks to their time spent in a top-notch neonatal unit, they came home healthy and were soon thriving. So I know how valuable it is to have a NICU at the medical center."

"Jennifer Walker's twins? Are you talking about Kaylee and Kevin?"

Catherine nodded. "I used to be Jenn's roommate in New York."

"So that's how you met Ray," Selena surmised, "through Dan and Eva."

Uh-oh. That hadn't been part of the story she and Ray had created last night, but it was the truth, so she nodded in agreement. "That's how we first met, of course. But nothing came of it. Then we ran into each other again in Houston six months ago. He attended one of my performances and came to visit me backstage—just to say hello. He asked me to have a drink with him, and one thing led to another."

"You're a performer?" Selena asked.

"I sing a little and dance." Catherine thought it might be a good idea to downplay the acting.

"That's wonderful. Our next benefit is a talent show, so it would be nice if you took part in it."

Catherine was at a loss, and she glanced at Ray, hoping he'd toss her a lifeline of some kind.

"That's on the second Saturday of this month," Ray said. "Right?"

Selena nodded. "Can we count on you to perform?"

Good grief, Ray was leaving it up to her. But then again, she supposed that was only fair. He couldn't very well schedule her every waking moment.

"I'll see what kind of act I can come up with," Catherine said.

"That's great," Selena said. "Clarissa Eubanks is in charge of the talent show. I'll tell her to call the mayor's office for contact information."

"I'll make it easy on both of you," Ray said. "Catherine's staying with me."

They made the usual small talk for a while, then Selena saw someone else she needed to greet.

"Congratulations on your engagement," she said as she prepared to walk away. "I hope you'll be very happy together."

"Thank you. I'm sure we will." Catherine turned to Ray and blessed him with a lover's smile, which he returned in full force.

For a moment, as their gazes zeroed in on each other again, something she couldn't quite define passed between them, something warm and filling.

He reached to take her hand again, and as his fingers wrapped around hers, the shattered edges of her heart, which had been damaged by Erik's deceit, melded into one another, as if beginning a much-needed healing process.

Coming to Brighton Valley had been a good idea, she decided.

With her hand tucked in Ray's, reinforcing whatever tentative bond they'd forged just moments ago, her past turned a brand-new corner, revealing a future rife with promise and possibilities.

And for one brief moment in time, she could almost imagine that future including Ray Mendez.

Ever since Ray had agreed to take the job as the interim mayor of Brighton Valley, he'd spent more time at various benefits, ribbon-cutting ceremonies and dinner meetings than he'd imagined possible.

In fact, just thirty-six hours ago, he'd dreaded attending this very event.

Not that he didn't fully support the building of a new neonatal intensive care unit. He did, but he'd been waking up each morning at four, just so he could tend to his personal business commitments, as well as the political obligations that now filled his calendar.

Yet tonight, with lovely Catherine on his arm, the hospital benefit had not only been tolerable, but surprisingly pleasant.

Of course, now as the evening was winding down, he and Catherine had become separated once again. Usually they'd split up due to someone wanting to speak to him privately about one matter or another. But a couple of times, someone else had whisked Catherine away to introduce her to somebody she "just had to meet."

However, they'd always managed to find each other in the midst of the milling crowd.

Even from across the room, their gazes would meet. And when they did, Catherine would look at Ray with a lover's yearning. At least, that's the way it felt to him.

The first time it had happened, he'd been so unbalanced by the expression on her face that his breath had caught. But after a while he'd actually come to look forward to their eye contact.

What was with that?

He knew that their so-called romance was all an act, but he'd gotten so caught up in their performance that he'd found himself seeking her out, just to catch her eye.

And there she was now, standing next to a potted palm, talking to one of the doctors' wives. And here it came—the glance his way, the look, the smile, the expression that announced she would much rather be curled up in bed with him.

She was good. *Really* good. And it was all he could do to remember that they'd only just met, that she was his employee, that they hadn't slept together—and that they would never even consider it.

Well, hell. Okay, so he probably would consider it—if it ever came to that. But it wouldn't.

The affectionate glances, the touches, were all just for show. Things would be much different when they returned to his apartment.

So why was all that phony longing driving him nuts now?

Because she was such a good actress that he was buying it all—hook, line and sinker. How was that for bad luck and a lousy roll of the dice?

Still, he planned to take one last opportunity to claim his fiancée this evening. Then he'd take her home and end it all.

After checking his wristwatch and deciding now was the time, Ray made his way across the room to where Catherine was speaking to Margo Reinhold, the wife of one of the city councilmen.

"Your fiancée and I have been talking," Margo said to Ray. "I suggested that she join the Brighton Valley Women's Club. We're having a luncheon and fashion show next month, so it would be a fun meeting to attend. We're also looking for more models, so I hope she'll consider volunteering for that, as well."

There was no guarantee Catherine would still be in town this summer, so she couldn't very well commit to anything that far in advance without letting someone down.

Realizing her dilemma and seeing the indecision in her eyes, Ray stepped in to help. "I'm sure Catherine would love to join you ladies, but she has plans to…take a cruise with a couple of her girlfriends."

"Oh, yes," Catherine said, taking the baton he'd passed. "When is the fashion show?"

"It's on August the tenth."

Catherine's expression fell—just as if she were shattered that her previously made plans wouldn't allow her to take part in the event.

"Wouldn't you know it?" she said. "That's the day I set sail for the Caribbean."

"I'm so sorry to hear that," Margo said. "But there's always next year."

"Oh, of course." Catherine tossed Ray another one

of those bright-eyed, I-love-you grins. Or maybe it was one of those saved-by-the-bell smiles.

"Since you won't be leaving until mid-August," Margo continued, "maybe you'd like to help with the high school dance recital. It's on the last Saturday in July. I'm sure the young people would love to have some advice from a pro."

Had Catherine told Mary that she was a dancer? And a professional? Or had Selena Ramirez spread the word?

Ray supposed it was okay that the news was out, but something told him they'd better go over their story again so they didn't get mixed up and tell on themselves.

"I'd love to work with the kids," Catherine said.

Now, wait a minute. Catherine was working for *him*. How was she going to schedule practices at the high school when he might have need of her? And what if…

Well, what if she decided to stick around in Brighton Valley indefinitely? What would happen when he decided to end…her employment?

Of course, that could become a problem whether she started volunteering in the community or not.

Catherine placed a hand on his arm. "You don't mind, do you, honey?"

Had she read something in his expression? If so, he hadn't wanted anyone to know he was a little uneasy about their future together in Brighton Valley.

"Of course I don't mind," he said.

The women chatted a moment longer, then Margo handed Catherine a business card with her contact information. "Give me a call sometime tomorrow, and I'll schedule a meeting between you and the dance teacher at the high school."

At that point, Ray decided it was time to cut out. Who knew what else Margo had up her sleeve or what she might try to rope his pretty fiancée into?

"Are you ready to go home?" he asked Catherine.

"Yes, I am." Then she slipped her arm through his and said goodbye to Margo.

Five minutes later they were in his Cadillac Escalade and headed back to his apartment.

"Something tells me you didn't want me to volunteer to work with the dance recital," she said.

"It just took me by surprise, that's all."

"Why?"

He glanced across the seat and saw her studying him, her brow furrowed.

"I don't know," he said. "I'd hate to see you get more involved with the locals than you have to."

"Actually, I'd love to work with the kids. It will be a way for me to pay it forward."

"I don't understand."

After a beat, she said, "I grew up in a family that was both large and dysfunctional. Music was my escape from the noise and hubbub. I would have loved to have taken dance or piano lessons when I was a child, but my dad was chronically unemployed, and my mom used to spend her extra cash on beer and cigarettes for the two of them. So there wasn't any money available for the extras."

"So how'd you become a dancer?"

"In high school, I chose every music, dance or

drama class I could fit into my schedule. The teachers insisted I had a natural talent, and after a while I began to believe them. I also knew that an education was my way out of the small town where we lived, so I studied hard and landed a scholarship at a small liberal arts college in the Midwest."

"And from there you decided to go to New York?"

"In a way. I met Jenn Walker at college, and she insisted that we try our luck on Broadway. But it was Miss Hankin, my high school dance teacher, and Mr. Pretz, the choral director, who convinced me that I could actually have a career doing what I loved."

So that's what she meant by paying it forward. She wanted to encourage other talented students to reach for their dreams. He had to admire that, he supposed.

"Do you miss it?" he asked. "Being on Broadway?"

"Yes, although I was ready for a break."

Dan had mentioned that she was recovering from a bad relationship. And now that Ray knew her better, he was curious about the details. And about the guy who'd broken her heart.

"Why did you need to get away?" he asked.

She paused for the longest while, then said, "The man I was involved with turned out to be a jerk. So I wanted to distance myself for a while."

"From him?"

"And from everything that reminded me of him."

She didn't say any more, and he didn't want to pry. After all, he'd had his own ways of shutting Heather out of his life after their split. So who was he to criticize someone else's way of dealing with a bad and painful situation?

After he pulled into the parking lot in back of the drugstore, he found a space and turned off the ignition.

When Catherine reached for the handle to let herself out, he said, "Hold on. I'll get it for you." Then he slid out from behind the wheel, went around to the passenger side and opened the door for her.

"I could have gotten it," she said. "There's no one around who'd see me do it."

"We don't need an audience for me to be polite."

She graced him with a moonlit smile. "Then thank you."

A shade in one of the upstairs windows opened, letting a soft light pour out from the apartment over Caroline's Diner.

Apparently they weren't entirely alone and unnoticed.

As they started back across the dimly lit parking lot, Catherine's ankle wobbled, and she reached for Ray to steady herself.

As her fingers pressed into his forearm, setting off a surge of hormones in his bloodstream, he asked, "Are you okay?"

"Yes. I stepped in an uneven spot and lost my balance."

"Those high heels look great on you, but it's got to be tough walking in them, especially out here."

"Yes, it is." Still gripping his arm, she looked up at him. And as she did so, their gazes met—and held.

There it went again, that rush of attraction. And while he knew whatever they were feeling for each other was purely sexual, he couldn't help basking in it longer than was wise.

Then, as one heartbeat lapsed into a second and a third, he reached for her waist.

"We've got an audience," he whispered, making an excuse to hold her, to draw her close.

He doubted that was really the case, though. But he didn't care. All he wanted to do right this moment was to extend the act they'd been playing a little while longer. To push for just a bit more of that heated rush.

To maybe even push for another brief kiss…

As his blood began to race, he didn't think one that was brief would be quite enough.

Besides, he told himself, a kiss from Catherine, albeit a phony one, just might help him forget all the crap Heather had put him through.

Oh, what the heck. Who was he trying to kid? He wanted to kiss Catherine senseless—even if he'd pay for it later.

So he lowered his mouth to hers.

Chapter Four

The last thing Catherine expected this evening was for Ray to kiss her goodbye while they stood in the parking lot behind his apartment.

Not that she minded.

In fact, as she stepped right into his arms, her heart raced in anticipation as if she'd been waiting all evening to get her hands on him.

And maybe, somewhere deep inside, that's just what she'd been doing, because the moment their lips touched, the kiss, which she assumed was also a thank you for a job well done, intensified.

As tongues met, their breaths caught and desire sparked, turning something that began tender and sweet into something heated and sexual.

Before long, Catherine wasn't so sure who ought to be thanking or praising whom.

In fact, right this moment, all she wanted to do was to kiss Ray back and let nature run its course. And if truth be known, she wasn't doing this for the benefit of any neighbors who might be watching.

No, her motive was a bit more selfish than that.

Over the years, she'd kissed quite a few men—most of them her costars on stage. And not a single one of those kisses had come anywhere near to moving her as much as Ray's did.

She supposed this was a nice perk that went along with the job she'd been hired to do.

As the kiss ended, Ray placed a hand on her cheek. "You were great tonight."

He'd been *great,* too—especially right now.

Somehow, she managed an unaffected smile. She'd planned to thank him and tell him it had been easy, yet as his gaze settled on hers and his fingers trailed along her cheek, she found it difficult to speak.

On the other hand, his eyes were speaking volumes to her—if she could trust them. Maybe she was misreading something that was merely appreciation for affection.

The acting was over for tonight, wasn't it?

Sometimes, when she really got into a role, she became the character she portrayed. Is that what was happening now? Had she actually become Mendez's fiancée for the past couple of hours?

If so, she'd better shake that role on her drive back to the ranch.

"Well," she said, finding the words to segue back to reality. "I guess I'd better go. I don't want Dan and Eva worrying about me."

"I hate to have you drive back to the ranch this late at night. The road isn't well lit, and some of those curves are tough to make in the daylight."

So what was he suggesting?

"You're more than welcome to stay in town with me," he added. "We can call the Walkers and tell them you'll be bringing the car back in the morning."

He wanted her to spend the night with him? She probably ought to be a little concerned by his expectations, yet she didn't find the idea of a sleepover all that out of line. And she wasn't sure why.

The kiss maybe? The temptation to see where another one might lead?

No, she needed to keep things a little more professional than that.

"Thanks for the offer," she said, "but I think I can make the drive without any problems. If I'd had more to drink than club soda, I might take you up on it."

Still, in spite of the decision she'd made, Catherine knew it wouldn't take much of an argument from Ray for her to call Eva and tell her there'd been a change of plans. Her knees were still wobbly from the kiss. And the chemistry the two of them shared—on or off the stage—promised to be explosive.

"Just for the record," he added. "I'll sleep on the sofa and you can have the bed."

"That's tempting," she admitted. And not only because she was tired and didn't want to make the drive back to the ranch.

"Then what's holding you back?"

The truth? Not trusting herself when her senses were still reeling from that last kiss.

Instead, she said, "I don't like to change plans after they've been made, but I'll keep your offer in mind next time—assuming there'll be another event we need to attend together."

"It's going to take more than a couple of sightings for people to realize I'm engaged."

He was probably right.

"So what's next on the agenda?" she asked.

"How about lunch tomorrow? We can meet at City Hall around noon, then walk a couple of blocks to an Italian restaurant that just opened up. The owner's grandfather is a member of the city council, and I'd like to be supportive of a new local business endeavor."

"All right. I'll see you then."

She started toward the parked minivan, and Ray followed. When she reached the driver's door, he placed his hand on her shoulder. She turned, and as their eyes met, she sensed another goodbye kiss coming her way.

"Just in case someone's watching from one of the apartment windows," he said, as he slipped his arms around her.

Yet as their lips met, she had a feeling he would have kissed her a second time tonight, even if no one was looking down at them.

And if that had been the case, she would have let him.

The chemistry between them was much stronger than she'd anticipated, which might prove to be a real problem for her in the very near future.

The handsome Brighton Valley mayor was paying her to keep the single women at bay—not to join their ranks.

Sofia, one of the younger Walker twins, had awakened with an earache. So Eva had needed her car to drive the child to the pediatrician, which meant Catherine's only mode of transportation was one of the ranch pickups.

So, after getting directions to the Brighton Valley City Hall, an ornate brick building that the town fathers had built nearly a hundred years ago, Catherine drove into town to meet Ray for lunch.

As the beat-up old pickup chugged down Main Street, past Caroline's Diner and the other quaint little shops, Catherine held tight to the steering wheel, looking for town square and the public parking lot Dan had told her about.

Sure enough, it was right where he'd told her it would be. Once she'd found the automatic dispenser and paid for the two-hour minimum, she took the ticket back to the pickup. Then she crossed the street, entered the hundred-year-old brick building and made her way to a reception desk, where a middle-age woman with graying hair sat.

"Can I help you?" the woman asked.

Catherine offered a friendly smile. "I'm here to see Ray Mendez."

The woman's pleasant expression faded. "Do you have an appointment?"

"Not exactly. I came to have lunch with him."

"You don't say." The woman arched a brow, as if

she found that hard to believe. "I'm not sure if he's available. I'll have to give him a call."

Did she treat every visitor this way?

Catherine crossed her arms and shifted her weight to one hip. "Tell him that Catherine Loza is here."

The woman lifted the telephone from its receiver, then pushed an intercom button. When someone on the other end answered, she brightened. "Hello, Mayor. It's Millie. There's a young woman named Catherine here to see you."

Millie's smile faded, and her eyes widened.

"Your...fiancée?" She took another gander at Catherine, her expression softening. "Of course. I'll tell her you'll be right down."

Millie hung up the phone, then offered Catherine a sheepish grin. "I'm *so* sorry, Ms. Loza. It's just that I had no idea he... That you..."

"That's okay." Catherine lifted her left hand and flashed the diamond. "We haven't told many people yet."

"Still, I'm sorry. I didn't mean to be rude. It's just that I was asked to screen his calls and his visitors."

"I understand," Catherine said, realizing that Ray hadn't been exaggerating when he'd said the single women in town were making it difficult for him to get any work done.

Millie pointed to a row of chairs near her desk. "You can have a seat, if you'd like. But he said he'd be right down."

"Thank you."

Within moments Ray came sauntering down the

hall, a dazzling smile stretched across his face. "Hi, honey. Did you have any trouble finding the place?"

"No, not at all."

They kissed briefly in greeting, then Ray turned to the receptionist and said, "Thanks, Millie. I see you met Catherine. What do you think?"

"I think the local girls are going to be broken-hearted, especially when they realize they can't compete with the future Mrs. Mendez." Millie chuckled. "And once word gets out, it'll make my job easier. Now I won't have to stretch the truth and come up with excuses for you anymore."

"I guess my engagement is a win-win for all of us." Ray placed a hand on Catherine's back. "Are you ready to go, honey?"

"Whenever you are."

Ray took her by the hand, and after a two-block walk, they crossed the street to a small restaurant that offered curbside dining under the shade of a black awning.

"It's a nice day," Ray said. "Why don't we sit outside?"

"That sounds good to me."

After Ray told the hostess their preference, they were led to a linen-draped table and handed menus.

Ray held Catherine's chair as she took her seat. Then he sat across from her.

"I heard the manicotti was pretty good," he said.

Catherine scanned the menu, tempted to choose the pasta, but knowing she didn't need the carbs when she wasn't having regular workouts each day.

"What looks good to you?" Ray asked.

"I'd like the vegetarian antipasto salad—the oil and vinegar on the side. And a glass of water with lemon."

"That's it?"

"Yes, but I might try to steal a bite of whatever you're having—as long as it's high in carbs and covered in cheese."

He tossed her a boyish grin. "Be my guest."

Fifteen minutes later, after several of the townspeople stopped to say hello to the mayor and were pleasantly surprised to meet his "future bride," the waiter brought out their meals.

"Can I get you anything else?" the young man asked.

"No, this is fine for now." Ray glanced down at the lasagna he'd ordered. "I had no idea the servings would be this large. I'll give you half of it."

"Oh, no you don't. I just want a taste."

Ray cut off a good size chunk anyway, placed it on a bread plate, then passed it to her.

It was, she decided, just the kind of thing that lovers and friends did while eating. Yet she hadn't given their roles any thought when she'd asked to sample his meal.

Were they becoming friends?

Before she would even risk pondering the idea of them ever becoming lovers, she asked, "Do you have anything special on the calendar this week?"

"There's a community barbecue in the town square on Saturday afternoon. Besides having the best rib eye you've ever tasted, they'll have a pie-eating contest and a line-dance competition."

That sounded like fun. "What's the dress code?"

"I suppose you'd call it country casual, with denim being the only requirement."

"I can handle that." Catherine cut into the lasagna Ray had given her with a fork and took a bite. The minute it hit her mouth, she wished she'd agreed to split their meals.

"Do you have any Western boots?" Ray asked.

"No. Do I need a pair?"

"Not really. You'll be fine in jeans."

Maybe Eva would have a pair she could borrow. She'd ask her as soon as she got home.

They ate in silence for a while, and when Catherine reached for her glass of water, she caught Ray staring at her.

"What's wrong?" she asked.

"Nothing."

She didn't believe him.

Finally, he said, "You're a good sport."

She always tried to be. But something told her his comment held a deeper meaning. "What makes you say that?"

"Because you're a big-city girl. All this country-bumpkin stuff has to be pretty foreign to you. Are you that good of an actress?"

She laughed. "I'm a pretty good actress, but I wasn't always a big-city girl. I grew up in a small town in New Mexico, although it wasn't anything like Brighton Valley."

"You mentioned that to me before, but I still have trouble imagining you as anything other than a big-city girl."

"Why is that?"

He shrugged. "The way you carry yourself, I suppose. And because of your background on the Broadway stage."

"I've spent the past ten years surrounded by bright lights and skyscrapers, but that wasn't always the case."

"What was it like growing up in a small New Mexico community?" he asked.

"It was dry, hot and dusty for the most part. And I couldn't wait to leave it all behind."

He took a bite of garlic bread. "What about your family? Do they still live there?"

"A few of them do. My dad died when I was twelve, and my mother passed on about five years ago. Most of my siblings cut out the minute they turned eighteen, just like I did."

"*Most* of them? How many brothers and sisters do you have?"

"There were seven of us—three boys and four girls."

"I was an only child," he said. "I always wondered what it would have been like to have had siblings."

"Big families aren't always what they're cracked up to be. Mine was pretty loud and dysfunctional, and so I escaped through reading or listening to music."

"Is that when you decided to be an actress?"

She'd been gone so long and traveled so far, that whenever she looked back on those days, it was hard to believe she'd ever been that lonely girl with big dreams.

"I knew that an education was my only way out of

that town—and school provided the lessons I wanted. So I studied hard and landed a scholarship."

"At the college where you met Dan's sister?"

"Yes. Jennifer was determined to perform on Broadway, and her dreams were contagious. I began to think that I might be able to make the cut, too."

"And you did." He smiled, his eyes beaming as though he was proud of her.

Her heart skipped a beat at his belief in her, at his pride in her accomplishment. She hadn't had a cheerleader since Jenn died. And while Dan and Eva had always liked hearing about her successes, she'd never been able to share her failures with them in hopes of getting a pep talk.

She offered Ray a wistful smile. "After we graduated from college Jenn and I moved to New York, rented a small apartment in the Bronx and then tried out for every off-Broadway play or musical available. In time, we began to make names for ourselves, first with bit parts, then with an occasional lead role."

"Sounds like the perfect world—at least, for you."

"Yes and no. When Jennifer got pregnant with the twins and feared she'd have to call it quits, I was afraid I couldn't make it on my own. Not because I didn't have the talent, but Jenn was the one with the determination and the perseverance, the one who kept me going when things didn't work out as hoped or planned. So I offered to support her any way I could—*if* she'd stay in New York."

"Support? You mean financially or with the kids?"

"Both. I had no idea how difficult it would be to bring home two newborns."

"I'll bet that changed both of your lives."

It certainly had. And in a good way. A lot of roommates might have had qualms about having crying babies in the house, but Catherine and Jennifer had become a team—and a family.

But then again, Catherine had suffered a lot of female problems in the past. Since she'd been told that having a child of her own wasn't likely, it was only natural that she grew exceptionally close to Kaylee and Kevin.

"It must have been tough when Jennifer died."

Catherine nodded. Just the thought of losing the young woman who'd been both her best friend and a better sister than the three she'd had brought tears to her eyes.

It might have been four years ago, but the grief sometimes still struck hard and swift.

She could still recall that awful day as though it had been yesterday. She'd been home watching the kids and practicing the lines for a new part in an off-Broadway production when the doorbell rang. And when she'd answered, she'd found an NYPD officer on the stoop, who'd told her the news: Jennifer had been killed while crossing a busy Manhattan street— struck by a car.

At that time, Jennifer and her brother Dan, the twins' only surviving relative, had been estranged. He'd been devastated to learn of his sister's death and had flown to New York to do whatever he could. But the twins weren't quite five years old and hardly knew him. So Catherine had volunteered to keep the children for a few months to help them through the grieving process and to allow them time to get to know their uncle better.

When the kids finally moved to Brighton Valley, Catherine had missed them terribly, but she knew it was for the best. Still, she called regularly and visited them in Texas as often as her work would allow— although it wasn't nearly as often as she would have liked.

"I'm sorry," Ray said. "I didn't mean to bring up something painful and turn your afternoon into a downer."

Catherine lifted her napkin and dabbed it under her eyes. "That's okay. It happens sometimes. We were very close. And I still miss her." Then she managed a smile. "I really don't mind talking about her. And I don't usually cry."

As Ray watched Catherine wipe the tears from her eyes, he regretted the questions that had stirred up her grief. He'd only wanted to learn more about her, to get to know her better.

If they'd actually been dating, if he'd had the right to quiz her about her past, it might have been different.

She glanced at the napkin, noting black streaks on the white linen.

"My mascara is running," she said.

"Just a bit."

"I probably look like a raccoon." She smiled through her tears, relieving the tension, as well as his guilt. "Excuse me for a minute. I'm going to find the ladies' room and see if I can repair the damages."

Catherine had no more than entered the restaurant when Ray spotted Beverly Garrison getting out of her parked car. Beverly was the president of her homeowners' association and made it a point to attend every city council meeting, whether the agenda had anything to do with her neighborhood or not.

When Beverly saw him, she brightened and waved. "You're just the one I wanted to see, Mayor. I have something to give you."

Then she reached into the passenger seat and pulled out a yellow plastic tub.

What the heck was in it? Margarine?

"I looked for you over at Caroline's Diner," she said, as she bumped her hip against the car door to shut it. "But you weren't there. Someone suggested I look for you here."

She headed for his table. "I brought you a treat."

"What is it?" Ray asked.

"Two dozen of the best homemade oatmeal-raisin cookies you've ever eaten in your life. My daughter baked a fresh batch this morning. Carol Ann is a little shy, so she asked me to give them to you."

As Ray glanced down at the yellow tub, Beverly reached for the lid, peeled it off and revealed a stack of cookies that certainly looked delicious.

"Thanks for thinking of *me*," he said, a little surprised that she'd go so far as to chase him down.

"Oh, it wasn't me." Beverly's hand flew up to her chest, as she took a little step back. "It was my *daughter*. You remember Carol Ann, don't you? She's the pretty blonde who showed up at the last city council meeting with me."

Ray remembered, but poor Carol Ann, who'd spent

most of the time with her nose stuck in a book, was neither pretty nor blond. At best, she was a rather non-descript woman with stringy, light brown hair. She was also in her forties, which meant she was five to ten years older than him.

Not that age was that big of an issue. But Ray wasn't looking for a date.

Of course, he didn't want to hurt the woman or her daughter's feelings, so he kept those thoughts to himself.

"You'll have to thank Carol Ann for me," he said.

"I can certainly do that, but why don't I give you her telephone number instead? That way, you can call her yourself. It'd be a nice thing for you to do."

Ray took a deep breath, then glanced to the doorway of the restaurant, where Catherine stood, watching the matchmaking mama do her thing.

Catherine's lips quirked into a crooked grin, clearly finding a little humor in the situation.

Beverly reached into her black vinyl handbag and pulled out a pen and notepad. Then she scratched out Carol Ann's contact information, tore out the sheet she'd written upon and handed it to Ray. "Carol Ann has plenty of time on her hands these days. She and Artie Draper broke up a few months back, and…well, what with your recent divorce and all, I'm sure you understand how tough it is to get back into the dating world again."

It actually wouldn't be tough at all for him to start dating—if he were inclined to do so. There were single women ready, willing and able at every turn.

"I'll be sure to call Carol Ann and thank her for the

cookies," Ray said, getting to his feet and glancing to the doorway where Catherine stood by.

"That would be wonderful," Beverly said.

Taking her cue, Catherine approached the table.

"Beverly," Ray said, "I'd like to introduce you to my fiancée, Catherine Loza."

"How do you do," Catherine said. "Goodness, will you look at those yummy cookies."

Beverly's eyes widened and her lips parted as she ran an assessing gaze over Catherine. "I... I...um, didn't know you were engaged, Mayor...."

"It's only been official for a few days," Catherine said with a gracious smile. "And we haven't made any formal announcements."

Beverly took a step back, then fingered the top button of her blouse. "You know, I can probably thank Carol Ann for you, Mayor. There's probably no need for you to call her. She's pretty shy. And well, I'd hate to see her embarrassed. She...uh...."

"I understand," Ray said. "I wouldn't want to cause her any discomfort, especially after her recent breakup. But please give her my best. Tell her the right guy will come along. And before she knows it, she'll be happy again."

"Well," Beverly said, nodding toward her car. "I really need to get going. I have a lot of errands to run."

"Thank you for the cookies," Ray said. "Do you want me to return the container?"

"No, don't bother. You can just recycle it when you're through." Then she turned and strode to her car.

Ray pulled out Catherine's chair, and when she took a seat, he followed suit.

Once Beverly had closed her car door and backed out of her parking space, Ray glanced across the table, his gaze meeting Catherine's.

"See what I mean?" he asked. "That kind of thing happens to me all the time. And most of them don't know how to take a polite no for an answer."

"Well, hopefully, once word gets out that you're taken, you won't have to deal with those kinds of distractions anymore."

That was his plan. Having a hired fiancée seemed to be working like a charm, thank goodness. Although he had to admit, another actress might not have been able to pull it off with Catherine's grace and style.

Ray studied the beautiful blonde as she ate the last of her salad.

The sunlight glimmered in her hair, making the strands shine like white gold... The teal-colored blouse she wore made her blue-green eyes especially vivid today.

While in the restroom, she'd reapplied her mascara, as well as her pink lipstick.

Damn, she was attractive. And not just because of her appearance. In a matter of two days, she'd added something to his life—smiles, camaraderie...

Of all the women he'd met since his split from Heather, Catherine seemed to be the only one who might not complicate things.

Of course, she was an actress, so who knew if he was seeing the real Catherine. She also lived—and no doubt thrived—in Manhattan, which was worlds away from Brighton Valley.

Still, if things were different...

If he could trust that the woman who'd revealed herself to him was real…

If she were a normal, down-home type…

If she planned to escape the city lights and excitement and move to a small Texas town…

…then Ray would be sorely tempted to ask her out on a real date.

Chapter Five

On Saturday afternoon Catherine climbed into the same old ranch pickup she'd driven before and headed for Ray's apartment, but she wasn't sure if she would make it or not. Each time she stopped at an intersection, the engine sputtered and chugged as though it might stall at any moment.

Thankfully, she reached the alley behind the drugstore and parked in the lot next to a battered green Dumpster.

Before climbing out of the cab, she reached into her purse, pulled out her cell and called Dan.

"I'm sorry to bother you," she said, "but there's something wrong with the pickup."

"Are you stranded along the road?"

"No, I made it. But I'm not sure if I'll be able to get home or not."

He paused a moment, then said, "The ranch hands have all left for the day. And I'm still waiting for the vet. But I'll try to get out there as soon as I can."

Dan had a broodmare that was sick. And earlier this morning, while climbing on the corral near the barn, Kevin had fallen down and sprained his ankle, which was why Dan, Eva and the kids wouldn't be coming to the town barbecue.

"Don't give it another thought," Catherine said. "I just wanted to let you know. I'll ask Ray to look under the hood. And I'll also have him bring me home this evening."

"Don't bother asking Ray to look at the truck," Dan said. "As long as it won't put you in a bind or strand you in town, you can leave it right where it is. I'll call a towing service and have it brought home on Monday."

After she ended the call, Catherine got out of the pickup and crossed the parking lot. She'd borrowed a pair of cowboy boots from Eva, as well as faded jeans and a blue-and-white gingham blouse. She was certainly going to fit right in with the other Brighton Valley residents today, which ought to please Ray.

A smile tugged at her lips as she climbed the stairs to the small apartment, then used the key Ray had given her. She was a few minutes early, so once she was inside, she made herself at home—just as he'd told her to do.

The sparsely furnished apartment, while clean, tidy and functional, lacked any artwork on the walls or accent colors. She was tempted to pick up a couple of throw pillows, something to brighten up the place and make it a bit homier. But she supposed it didn't matter. Ray stayed here only on the nights he didn't want to drive all the way back to the ranch.

Catherine turned on the television. Then after finding the Hallmark channel, she took a seat on the brown leather sofa and watched the last half of a romantic comedy about a woman who was snowbound in a cabin with her ex-husband.

It wasn't until the ending credits began to roll that she heard another key in the lock, alerting her to Ray's arrival.

"I'm sorry I'm late," he said as he closed the door and stepped into the small living area that opened up to a kitchen and makeshift dining room. "I meant to get here sooner, but I was at a funeral of an old friend of my parents, and his widow asked me to meet with her and her attorney."

"Please don't apologize." Using the remote, she shut off the power on the television, then got to her feet. "I'm so sorry to hear that."

"Thanks. It wasn't a surprise. He'd been sick for a long time, so it was probably for the best." He loosened his tie.

Not only was Ray a successful rancher, he was also a loyal friend, which Catherine found admirable. No wonder he'd been elected to the city council and appointed mayor.

"Look at you," he said, breaking into a smile. "You're going to be the prettiest cowgirl at the barbecue."

Catherine didn't know about that, but she thanked him just the same.

"I need to change into something more appropriate," he said. "I'll only be a minute or two."

She knew he'd planned to be home a lot sooner than this. "Is there anything I can do to help? I know you'd wanted to arrive early."

"I was going to welcome everyone before the music started, but that's not going to happen now. I'll just have to do that at the halfway point." His steps slowed. "In fact, I'm even going to take time to get a drink of water."

"Is your life always like this?" Catherine asked as she returned to her seat on the sofa. "Do you run from one event or meeting to another?"

"Yep. That's pretty much the way each day goes."

She smiled. "I'll have to keep that in mind if I ever decide to run for public office."

"Actually," he said, removing his jacket, "I never planned on going into politics, but a few of my friends and neighbors—including Dan Walker—had been urging me to run for the city council. I'd put them off for a while, but…"

"Now here you are," she said, "the mayor of Brighton Valley."

"The *interim* mayor," he corrected. "I'm covering for Jim Cornwall, remember?"

"Are you sorry you took on the extra work?" she asked.

"I really don't mind the job itself. The biggest problem I have is balancing all of my other responsibilities."

"Such as…?"

"The day-to-day duties on my ranch, as well as

the new horse-breeding operation I'm just starting up with Dan." He blew out a sigh, and his shoulders seemed to slump a bit. "I hate leaving others to do the work I should be doing myself. And it's not easy being pulled in a hundred different directions. But I can handle it. Besides, now that you've stepped in as my 'fiancée,' things are a lot easier. I don't have to fend off the single ladies in town."

"That surprises me."

"What does?" He hung his jacket on the back of one of the dinette chairs. "That the women are interested in me?"

"No, not that." Goodness, not *that*. The man was successful, well-respected, personable and drop-dead gorgeous. "I'm just a little surprised that you're not the least bit interested in dating."

"I don't have time for a relationship. And even if I did, I'm not ready to get involved in another one."

If that was the case, then his ex-wife must have done a real number on him—just as Erik had done to her.

"Not that it's really any of my business," she said, "but why aren't you ready to start dating?"

"My divorce got ugly." He strode to the kitchen area, pulled a glass from the cupboard, then filled it with water from the tap. "And when the one person in the world you depend on to have your back kicks you in the ass instead…well, even a cowboy isn't too eager to get back in the saddle again."

She knew exactly what he meant. That's why she was in Brighton Valley these days, rather than in Manhattan.

After Ray had quenched his thirst and put the empty glass in the sink, Catherine said, "You mentioned that your divorce got ugly. I assume your marriage started out all right. When did things go south?"

"Probably after the first few weeks. But our relationship was wrong from the get-go. And it's my fault for not realizing that."

Catherine should have seen Erik's flaws, too, but love—or whatever she'd felt for him—had blinded her to them. She'd not only been hurt, but she'd felt pretty stupid, too. So it was nice to know she wasn't the only one who'd been snowballed by someone she'd cared about, someone she'd trusted.

"What clues did you miss?" she asked.

"First of all, Heather was a city girl who didn't like living on a ranch. And I was crazy for thinking she'd eventually get used to it." He clucked his tongue and shook his head. "She was also selfish and greedy. I'd noticed it going in, I suppose. But I hadn't realized just how bad it really was." He pointed to Catherine's left hand. "When I asked Heather to marry me, she turned up her nose at the ring you're wearing. I know it isn't much, but she couldn't see the value in it—the vows made and kept over the years."

Catherine lifted her finger, studied the small stone. Again she thought about Ray's grandmother, the woman who'd worn it and cherished the love and the promises it had represented.

"I should have taken a step back and reconsidered my proposal at that point," Ray said as he left the kitchen area, "but I stuck the ring in the safe, then went out and purchased a two-carat diamond for her instead."

Catherine had always believed there were two sides to every story—until she'd met Erik and fallen for his lies. So she found herself disliking Ray's ex-wife, even though they'd never met.

"Were the two of you ever happy?" she asked.

"At first, but once we got home from our honeymoon, the complaints started. And it became clear that she hated everything about my life—and me, too. Before long, she was spending more time in the city than she was in Brighton Valley. The day we split, she finally admitted that she was having an affair with a plastic surgeon."

"I'm sorry."

"About the divorce? Don't be. It was for the best. Trouble was, she hired a high-priced attorney out of Houston, and even though I'd expected to pay a hefty settlement, I hadn't been prepared for a legal battle. Each time I thought we'd reached some kind of agreement, she'd ask for something else. The whole thing dragged on for nearly two years."

Catherine didn't know what to say. Another *I'm sorry* seemed not only redundant but inadequate.

"I'm just glad it's finally over," he said. "So you can see why I'd be hesitant to get involved with someone else again—especially a woman who's only interested in me because she thinks I'd make a good catch."

Ray Mendez would make a *wonderful catch* for any woman, so Catherine could certainly understand why every Tamara, Diane and Mary in town was trying her best to snag his attention or set him up with someone she knew.

Yet Ray had a lot more going for him than his financial portfolio and political standing in the community. And he deserved a woman who'd be true blue and a helpmate to him.

"Dan said you'd been through a breakup, too," Ray said.

Catherine hadn't meant to bring up the subject. Goodness, she was trying to forget Erik and all he'd put her through. But after Ray's heartfelt disclosure, it seemed only fair to admit that she'd been hurt and disappointed, too.

"Last year I met a producer who'd recently moved to Manhattan from London. He asked me out, and we started dating. Before long, he promised me a starring role in the play he was producing, and I was thrilled. In fact, he also gave me an opportunity to invest in the production, which meant I'd reap some of the profit.

"For the first time in my life, I began to believe that I might finally be able to have it all—a successful career and a happy marriage. But he turned out to be a scam artist who ran off, taking the funding for a production that never came to pass."

"I'm sorry to hear that."

Catherine had not only been crushed and embarrassed by his deception, but she'd also lost a large chunk of her savings to the lying jerk.

"So you decided to get away for a while?" Ray asked.

That was about the size of it. She'd sublet her

brownstone for three months and flown to Texas to stay with Dan and Eva.

"I figured that Brighton Valley would be a great place to lick my wounds and to sort out my options," she admitted.

And while she was here, she'd use the downtime to allow her body to mend. Like many professional dancers, she'd suffered a couple of injuries that made it difficult for her to continue performing in musicals.

To be honest, she hoped to land more singing or acting roles from now on. But she'd deal with that once she got back to Manhattan.

In the meantime, she tossed Ray an appreciative smile. "And thanks to you, I'll not only be able to stay longer, I'll also be able practice my acting skills while I'm here."

"I'm glad to do my part. You've been a real godsend. If things continue to go well, I'll have to give you a bonus."

With finances being what they were, she could certainly use the extra cash, but she couldn't take any more money for doing a job that came so easily to her.

"That's not necessary," she said. "I get a lot of perks working for you."

"Such as…?"

"Meals and entertainment."

As their gazes met, as their time so far together came to mind, another perk crossed her mind: heart-spinning kisses that turned her every which way but loose.

Her cheeks warmed at the memory. Afraid to let him know what she was thinking, she turned away, walked several steps to the window and peered at the street below just so she could break eye contact.

"When do you plan to return to New York?" he asked.

"I don't know. In a couple of months, maybe. I don't have a return flight scheduled."

She liked knowing she could leave whenever she grew tired of being in Brighton Valley, although she found the rural Texas setting both quaint and restful. But she'd grown up in a small town and had found it to be stifling.

In Manhattan, she'd thrived and had finally become the woman she was meant to be.

"Well, I'd better get into my boots and jeans," he said, removing his wristwatch and leaving it on the dinette table, "or we'll end up arriving even later than we already are."

Minutes later, Ray sauntered into the living room in his Western wear, his Stetson in hand. His bright-eyed, sexy grin was so mesmerizing that Catherine couldn't help thinking that he made the perfect cowboy hero to play opposite her.

How did Brighton Valley's most handsome and eligible bachelor get better-looking each time she laid eyes on him?

"I'm sorry I kept you waiting," he said.

She offered him a breezy smile and said, "No problem," even though she could see a huge one looming on the horizon.

Ray had hired her to keep the local ladies from setting their romantic sights on him, and she had no reason to doubt that they'd respect the phony engagement.

Catherine would respect the role she was playing, too. And there was the problem.

As Ray opened the door for her, she grabbed her purse and proceeded downstairs. In a matter of minutes she'd be strolling along the street with the hottest cowboy in town.

She'd pretend to be in love with the handsome mayor, although it wouldn't take much acting on her part to feign her affection or her attraction to him.

No, the real difficulty would be in forgetting that it was all part of the act.

Ray and Catherine decided to walk to the community barbecue, since the town square was just down the street. In fact, it was so close that they'd barely stepped onto the sidewalk when they caught a hearty whiff of mesquite-grilled meat and heard the sound of bluegrass music.

"It sure smells good," Catherine said.

"Wait until you taste it. Brighton Valley goes all out for this event."

Ray, who'd been fighting the urge to hold her hand while they'd made the five-block walk, reached for it now.

It was all part of the act, he told himself. Yet there was something very appealing about Catherine. Something that made him happy to be with her.

Maybe it was the fact that she wasn't batting her eyelashes at him, that she wasn't delivering homemade cookies and hinting that she'd like more than a friendship.

Yeah, he told himself. That had to be it.

But as she slipped her hand into his, as their fingers threaded together, a burst of pride shot through him.

Or was it more than that?

Unwilling to let the possibility of anything "more" take root, he said, "I think you'll have a good time. Besides having the best barbecue food you've ever eaten, several of the local bands will be playing and trying to outdo each other as a way of promoting themselves for future parties and performances."

"Is it all bluegrass and country-western music?" she asked.

"For the most part. You'll hear some banjo groups and a couple of fiddlers. But there'll probably be some classic rock, too."

"It sounds fun."

He'd always liked attending the event, but something told him he was going to enjoy it a whole lot more with Catherine as his date.

Well, not a date in the classic sense of the word.

As they turned the corner and caught the first glimpse of the town square, Ray gave her hand a gentle squeeze. "Here we are."

The parklike area had already begun to fill with local residents, who stood in small groups on the grass or sat in some of the white chairs and tables they'd gotten from the party-rental company.

Near the courthouse, the Barbecue Pit, a local restaurant known for its great sauce, had set up an old-style chuck wagon, as well as a portable barbecue grill, where several men with white aprons watched the meat cook over mesquite chips.

Over by the restrooms, Charlie Biller's bluegrass band played their last set, as the Dave Hawkins Trio stood by, waiting to take their place on stage.

Now would be a good time for Ray to walk up to the microphone and welcome everyone to the event that had become one of the highlights of the year.

They'd barely stepped off the sidewalk and onto the grass when they were met by Buddy Elkins, one of the older city council members. Buddy was dressed in his cowboy finest—complete with boots, a silver buckle and a Stetson.

As recognition dawned, the silver-haired councilman headed straight for Ray with a big grin on his face. "I'd heard you snatched up the prettiest little gal in these parts, but I gotta tell ya', Mayor, the rumor mill didn't do this young lady justice. You really hit the jackpot this time."

Ray winked at Catherine, then released her hand so he could shake Buddy's. "You've got that right. I'm a lucky man. Catherine has renewed my faith in women."

That same surge of pride returned as Ray watched Buddy tip his hat to Catherine. "I'm pleased to meet you, ma'am."

She thanked him, then blessed him with a pretty smile.

Buddy elbowed Ray. "There'll be a hundred young men who'll be chomping at the bit to take your place—and a few my age who'd like to give you a run for your money. So you'd better treat her right."

"You can bet on it." Ray stole a glance at Catherine, and she gave him one of those starry-eyed smiles he'd suggested she throw his way every now and again. But this one shot right to his heart—or somewhere thereabouts. In fact, if he didn't know better, he'd think it was real.

Too bad it wasn't. He could get used to having a woman look at him like that—especially if the lady was her.

Shaking off the effects of their playacting, Ray said, "I'm going to head over to the stage and welcome people to the barbecue. But I'll be right back, Buddy. So don't try to steal my girl from me."

Buddy, who was nearing seventy, chuckled. "I'll keep my eye on her and chase off any riffraff who might not be as honorable as I am."

Ray brushed a kiss on Catherine's cheek, but as he did so, he caught a whiff of her floral scent, which taunted him to distraction. But he didn't dare stray from his task, so he excused himself and headed for the bandstand.

Along the way, several of the local townspeople stopped him to ask about one thing or another—but mostly to congratulate him on his engagement. For the first time in what seemed like ages, no one tried to hit on him or introduce him to the perfect woman.

Apparently the Brighton Valley residents had begun to realize that he'd already found her.

Of course, when it came to hired fiancées, he certainly had. Catherine was not only classy and sophisticated, but she also seemed to have a down-to-earth way about her.

Ray reminded himself that she was a talented actress who was able to immerse herself in a role. And even though a bucolic setting and small-town personalities held little appeal to a woman who'd moved on to the big city, Catherine appeared to be in her element and charmed everyone she met.

In fact, Ray felt a little bewitched by her, too.

When Charlie Biller, the leader of the bluegrass band, noticed Ray standing near the stage, he nodded to acknowledge him.

As soon as the song ended, the audience broke into applause. Charlie thanked them, then announced, "Let's all give a hand to Mayor Mendez."

Once Ray stood at the microphone, he welcomed everyone to the barbecue, then thanked the committee members who'd worked so hard to put on the event, as well as the local businesses and citizens who'd made donations of both money and goods.

"Before I turn the stage over to Dave and his trio," Ray said, "I'd like to take a minute to thank you for offering your best wishes on my engagement."

A brief hush fell on the crowd, followed by a gasp or two and some startled looks.

Ray scanned the grounds, looking for Catherine, finding her in the same place he'd left her. "Honey? Where are you?"

The townspeople, many of whom hadn't heard the news, began to crane their necks, seeking the woman in question.

Catherine, who wore a pretty smile, lifted her hand and fluttered her fingers. Then she blew Ray a little kiss.

Damn. She was good. And so *natural*....

So believable.

But Ray couldn't very well stand there and gawk at her like everyone else. So he said, "Let's get on with the show."

As the trio of banjo players took their place on-stage, Ray stepped onto the lawn, only to be stopped by Clyde Wilkerson, one of the local ranchers.

"I had no idea you were engaged," Clyde said. "When in the world did that happen? My wife was planning to invite you to dinner so she could introduce you to our niece."

"I kept things quiet until I popped the question and she said yes."

Clyde took another gander at Catherine. "Lucky you. She's certainly a pretty one."

"Yes, she is." Ray found himself craning his neck, looking for her. And wanting to make his way back to her.

"Where'd you find her?" Clyde asked.

"In Houston. I saw her dance on stage at the Yellow Rose Theater, and I knew right then and there that I had to meet her. We've been seeing each other for several months now."

"I don't suppose she has a sister," Clyde said. "I'd sure like to see my son Grady find a lady like that."

Catherine, who'd managed to break free of Buddy, made her way to where Ray and Clyde were standing. She offered Ray an I-missed-you-baby smile, then slipped her arm through his.

Trouble was, Ray had kind of missed her, too.

He supposed he ought to be glad his ploy was

working—and he was. The whole town square was abuzz with whispers about the mayor's new lady and nods of approval, indicating they were all clearly impressed by the match.

Thank goodness for that small miracle.

Some bachelors might find it nice to have nearly every single woman in town trying to catch their eye. And while Ray had spent more than his share of lonely nights during the months leading to his divorce and the two years after he and Heather had split, he'd put it all behind him now. And it grated on him to have anyone assume that he'd never be a whole man until he landed another wife, when that couldn't be any further from the truth.

Heck, even if he were the needy kind, he wasn't interested in complicating his life with romance until long after his job as interim mayor was finished. And to be honest, the jury was still out on whether he ever wanted another wife or not. His divorce had left him more than a little gun-shy when it came to trusting his heart to anyone again. So he wasn't going to give matrimony another try anytime soon.

Of course, it was a little weird and disconcerting to think that he'd not only had to pay through the nose to divorce the ex-wife who'd made his life a living hell, but that he was now paying a fake fiancée to keep his life simple and maintain his privacy.

On the other hand, he found himself enjoying Catherine's attentions far more than he could have imagined.

So he placed his hand on her lower back. "Come on, honey. Let's get something to eat."

They'd no more than taken a couple of steps when an old pickup started up, then backfired.

Catherine jumped. "What was that? A gunshot?"

Ray slipped his arm around her and smiled. "No, it was just an old truck that needs a tune-up."

"Oh, thank goodness." As they walked toward the chuck wagon, she leaned into him, just as if it was the most natural thing in the world to do.

And maybe it was.

"Speaking of old trucks," she said, "I completely forgot to mention this. Dan's pickup, which I drove into town today, isn't running very well. So I'm going to need a ride home this evening—unless you don't mind me sleeping on your sofa."

No kidding? Ray would love to have her stay the night with him in town. And she didn't need to take the sofa. She could sleep anywhere she liked.

"If you spend the night," he said, "I'll take you to Caroline's Diner for breakfast in the morning. The Brighton Valley Rotary is meeting in the back room, and that way, people will assume we're not only engaged but sleeping together."

It was kind of a lame excuse, especially since Ray hadn't even planned to attend the meeting. But if it meant having Catherine to himself this evening, then so be it.

"Sounds good to me."

It did? Was she feeling that comfortable with him, too? Or did spending the night just make her job easier?

The only way to find out for sure was to ask, and he wasn't about to do that.

They continued on to the chuck wagon and the spread of food that had been set out on long tables, but it took nearly twenty minutes to get there, thanks to all the folks who stopped them to offer their congratulations.

Each time it happened, Catherine lit up like a happy bride at her wedding.

Needless to say, the phony engagement was working beautifully, and Ray couldn't imagine anyone thinking that Catherine wasn't in love with "her man."

He supposed he ought to be pleased, but for some reason, he felt compelled to steal her away from the crowd, to find someplace quiet and romantic where they could spend the rest of the evening alone.

And he didn't dare contemplate why.

Chapter Six

As the sun set over Brighton Valley, black, wrought-iron gas lamps that had been spaced throughout the town square came on, bathing the parklike grounds in a soft glow.

An hour earlier, Ray had introduced Catherine to Shane and Jillian Hollister, then asked the couple to join them at their table when they ate dinner. Shane, who'd once been a detective with the Houston Police Department, had worked on Dan Walker's ranch prior to being appointed as the Brighton Valley sheriff.

Shane was off duty today, yet he continued to make the rounds, just as Ray did. But Catherine didn't mind fending for herself. She'd hit it off with Jillian. And she also enjoyed holding Mary Rose, the Hollisters' three-month-old daughter.

"It must be tough leaving the baby with a sitter while you do your student teaching," Catherine said.

"Yes, it is, but my grandmother recently moved to Brighton Valley and watches Mary Rose for me. In fact, Gram loves providing child care and even has her own little nursery set up. So I'm really fortunate in that respect."

Catherine studied the infant in her arms and smiled. "It seems like ages since I've held a little one."

"Did you have brothers and sisters?"

"Yes, but by the time I left for college, I was so eager to get a break from them that I didn't think I'd ever want to have kids of my own."

"Have you changed your mind?"

"I suppose," Catherine said wistfully, "but I've had a lot of female problems, including endometriosis. The doctor told me that I'd probably never conceive."

"I'm sorry to hear that," Jillian said.

"Me, too." Catherine glanced up and gave her an I've-accepted-it smile. "But the Walker twins have become the children I'll never have. After Kaylee and Kevin were born, I fell in love with them. And since their mother was my roommate, the kids lived with me for the first five years of their lives. So at least I've had the whole baby experience—times two."

Catherine glanced down at Mary Rose, realizing that holding someone else's child wasn't the same as holding her own.

The thought of adopting someday struck again, which was comforting. At least she had options available to her.

"You know," Jillian said, "my doctor, Selena Ramirez, is a great obstetrician/gynecologist. She was a resident at the Brighton Valley Medical Center, but started up her own practice last year. You might want to check with her and get a second opinion. She also treats infertility."

If Catherine were going to stay in town, she'd give it some thought. But she had no business even thinking about home and hearth and families at this point in her life.

Still, she scanned the town square, searching for Ray and finding him talking to Jillian's husband. As their gazes met, a warm feeling spread throughout her chest, setting off a yearning she couldn't quite explain.

What was that all about? It's not as though she and Ray actually had a future together.

Jillian glanced at the bangle watch she wore on her wrist, then sighed. "As much as I'd like to stay here, I need to take Mary Rose home. It's getting close to her bedtime."

Catherine took one last look at the precious infant in her arms, then handed her back to her mommy.

"I need to let Shane know I'm leaving," Jillian said. "That is, if I can find him."

"He's over there," Catherine said, pointing toward the chuck wagon, "talking to Ray."

"Oh, yes. I see them." Jillian reached for the diaper bag, then paused. "I hate to leave you sitting by yourself."

"Don't feel bad about that. I like sitting here, listening to the music." She'd also enjoyed talking to Jillian, as well as the various townspeople who occasionally stopped by to introduce themselves and to welcome her to Brighton Valley.

"Shane and I will be inviting you and Ray for dinner one day soon," Jillian said, as she prepared to leave.

"I'd like that." Catherine had found it easy to talk to Jillian. And the fact that she was also a friend of Eva's made it all the nicer.

"Hopefully, Ray will come back soon."

"I'm sure he will." Catherine offered her new friend a smile. "And even if he doesn't, I'm in no hurry to leave. I'm having a good time."

As Jillian crossed the lawn and approached her husband, Catherine watched her go. Once she'd reached Shane's side, Ray spoke to them both for a moment longer, then he softly stroked Mary Rose's dark hair before returning to Catherine's table.

"How are you holding up?" he asked as he took a seat beside her.

"I'm fine. How about you?"

"Winding down." He lifted his Stetson with one hand, then combed his fingers through his dark hair with the other. "It's been a long day, and I'd really like to say my goodbyes and get away from the crowd and all the noise."

It must have been especially tiring for him. Even though he wasn't being bombarded by matchmakers, a lot of people continued to drag him off to talk about a project or a problem they had.

"Will you be able to leave soon?" Catherine asked. "Or do you need to stay until it's over?"

"It's supposed to go on for another hour, but I don't need to stay that long."

As she studied him in the soft light created by one of the gas lamps, she noticed that his expression had turned serious, creating a furrowed brow.

Was something weighing on his mind? Or was he just tired, as he'd implied?

When his gaze caught hers, he seemed to shake the serious thoughts. "You've got to be worn to a frazzle."

"Not really." She'd been able to kick back and enjoy the day, but he hadn't been that lucky. He'd had to work.

In a sense, she supposed she'd been working, too. But being Ray's fiancée hadn't required much effort on her part. It had been an easy role to fall into. In fact, at times it felt as though the two of them were a real couple.

But even if it was real, long-distance relationships had two strikes against them already. Not that Ray had indicated he'd like to become involved in something like that.

As the country-western band began to play a slow and sultry love song, Catherine stood and reached out her hand to him. "Okay, Mr. Mayor. I've been patient long enough. You've been so busy with your civic duties that you haven't even gotten around to dancing with the woman you love, and I think it's high time you did."

He tilted his head slightly, then when he caught her wink, he smiled, slipped his hand into hers and let her lead him to the dance floor.

On the stage, an attractive young brunette vocalist sang "Breathe," the hit song that had earned Faith Hill a Grammy.

The local singer certainly wasn't as talented as Faith, but she gave it her all, and the other couples who'd gathered on the dance floor seemed to appreciate her efforts.

"I should have thought of this earlier," Ray whispered, as they walked across the lawn. "People are probably wondering why I haven't been courting my fiancée properly."

"I'm not so sure about that," she said, lowering her voice to match his. "We put on a believable act for them."

In fact, there'd been times throughout the day that she'd nearly forgotten that she really wasn't his lover, that he'd only hired her to play the part.

When they reached the dance floor, Catherine turned to Ray, whose smile had lit his face and completely chased away that furrowed brow.

"I'm not a bad dancer," he said as they came together, "for an amateur. But I'm sure you're used to guys with a lot more talent than I've got. So take it easy on me, okay?"

As she peered into his eyes and saw them sparkle with mirth, she returned his grin. "I'm not looking for any fancy footwork, Ray. All you need to do is sway to the music, and I'll follow your lead."

As he opened his arms, she stepped into his embrace, savoring the warmth of his body and the musky scent of his cologne.

It's an act, she told herself. But as she felt the strength of his arms, as they melded into one on the dance floor, she couldn't help wishing there was something more going on between them.

If things were different...

If she were going to stay in Texas indefinitely...

If she didn't have a career waiting for her in New York, directors who'd like to cast her again...

But how crazy was that? If she stayed in Brighton Valley, she'd have to give up all she'd ever wanted, all she'd worked so hard to achieve.

No, they just had this time together—today, tonight, next week. Who knew how long she'd stay in town? Who knew when the urge to return to the stage would strike?

The song, it seemed, ended all too soon. And as Ray released her, she hadn't been ready to let him go.

That is, until their eyes met and she spotted the intensity burning in his gaze.

Well, what do you know? The dance had affected him, too.

"Come on," he said, taking her by the hand. "Let's go home."

Her heart skipped a beat, then slipped into overdrive.

Home, he'd said. But right now, she'd follow him anywhere—no matter what role she was playing, even if she were merely being herself.

Ray had taken Catherine's hand when they'd walked off the dance floor, and he continued to hold it as they left the town square and headed back to his apartment.

He wasn't sure what he'd expected when he'd taken

her into his arms—just a run of the mill slow dance, he supposed. But when his hands had glided along the curve of her back and he'd drawn her close, there'd been more than a seductive tune and lyrics swirling around them.

No one ever told him that acting could be so much fun—or so arousing. He could almost imagine their phony romance taking a turn toward the real thing.

Would he ever find a woman like Catherine—or like the woman she was pretending to be?

Again, he wondered how much was acting and how much of it was genuine. After all, he was only human. And he'd been celibate for nearly two years.

Damn, had it really been that long?

He had no idea what to expect when they returned to his apartment—a good-night kiss or maybe one of appreciation? It was hard to say, but something told him that any kiss they shared was going to consume him with lust for the beautiful woman who had the ability to turn him inside out with just a smile.

Still, he was glad to know she'd be going home with him. Even if it meant one of them would be sleeping on the sofa.

As they walked down Main Street, which was quiet now that the stores had closed, their boot soles crunched along the sidewalk.

"There's something appealing about Brighton Valley," she said.

"I think so."

"How'd you like growing up here?"

He wasn't sure why she'd asked, but he gave her

an honest answer. "It was great. I can't imagine living anywhere else."

She seemed to think on that for a moment, then she nudged her arm against his. "You mentioned being an only child. That must have been nice—and peaceful. The house I grew up in was just one drama after another."

"My home life was nice and quiet, but it was lonely at times."

She smiled. "Sometimes people can be lonely in a crowd."

He supposed she might be right about that. "It wasn't so bad, though. My parents wanted me to socialize, so they let me invite plenty of friends to come to the ranch."

"Did you have any cousins?" she asked.

"Nope. It was just one set of grandparents, my folks and me. In fact, I was the only son of an only son."

"I'm sorry," she said.

"Don't be. It wasn't so bad." A smile tugged at Ray's lips, as he thought back to the loving home in which he'd grown up. "I was a late-in-life baby, whose birth was an answer to my mother's prayers. Needless to say, all the adults in my life doted on me."

Catherine's smile deepened, setting off her pretty dimples. "I'll bet they're proud of the man you've grown up to be."

"They were. They sat in the front row of every school play I was in, every Little League game I played. And they cheered, even if I messed up, telling me that it didn't matter."

"Do they live with you?" she asked. "I mean, it being a family ranch and all."

"No. My grandpa passed away when I was a junior in high school, and my dad died three years later. I lost my grandmother next, and my mom right before my thirtieth birthday."

"That's too bad. I'm sorry."

He was, too. "I guess that's the downside of having older parents. You usually lose them a lot sooner than most of your friends."

He sensed her grieving for him, and he appreciated the sentiment—whether sincere or not. Heather hadn't fully understood or sympathized with his loss—and she hadn't even tried to fake it. Instead, she'd thought he was lucky to have been the sole heir of the family ranch, the biggest spread in Brighton Valley and all the investments his family had accrued over two generations.

But he would have given it all up just to have his family still with him.

As they neared the drugstore, he realized they'd be at his apartment in no time at all and he found himself looking forward to having some time alone with the woman who was unlike any other he'd ever known.

"So what about school?" she asked. "Did you attend college?"

He wasn't sure what had triggered her curiosity, yet he didn't mind her interest in his past. So he said, "I went to Texas A and M."

There didn't seem to be any reason to mention that he'd graduated at the top of his class and received several job offers before his last semester—a couple in the Dallas area and one near Houston. He'd turned them down, though. Instead, he'd come home and taken over the family ranch, which he'd made even more successful than his grandfather and father had made it.

As they continued to hold hands and to make their way down the quiet, deserted downtown street, Ray relished the intimacy they shared.

"What about you?" he asked.

There wasn't much to tell—at least, when it came to her childhood—but Catherine supposed it was only fair that he quizzed her, too.

"I don't have too many good memories of growing up. By the time I graduated from high school, all I wanted to do was get on the first bus heading to Ohio."

"Ohio?" he asked.

"I had a scholarship to Crandall School of Fine Arts. It wasn't my first choice of colleges, but it had offered the best scholarship and was the farthest from home. So I jumped at it."

"And that's where you met Jenny Walker?"

She nodded. "Then we both moved to Manhattan."

Once she'd left New Mexico, she'd really begun to thrive in the college setting—and even more so in the metropolis, where she'd finally become the woman she was meant to be.

"I've never gone to New York," he said. "Brighton Valley must be a huge culture shock for someone used to a city that's open twenty-four hours a day."

"That's for sure."

Their boots continued to crunch on a light film of

grit on the sidewalk that lined the empty street, reminding her just how huge the difference was. Still, there was something appealing about the community, as well as the people she'd met so far.

When they reached the drugstore and the stairwell that led to Ray's apartment, his steps slowed. Then he withdrew his hand from hers and motioned for her to go first.

As she started up the lit steps, she wondered what the evening would bring. More disclosures, she supposed.

Would he kiss her again? Probably not. Once they were completely out of sight from any passersby, it wouldn't be necessary.

Still, she couldn't help but hope that he would, and by the time they reached his front door, her heart rate kicked up a notch.

Ray pulled out his keys, slipped them into the lock, then let her in. Once inside the small apartment, he hung his hat on the hook by the door.

She scanned the sparsely decorated living area, again tempted to do something to help him add a little color. In one of several small apartments inside of an old brownstone in Greenwich Village she called home, she'd done her best to brighten up the drab rooms by using vivid shades of red, yellow and blue, then adding a splash of purple here and there.

Even her furniture back home—a selection of black, glass and chrome—was modern in style.

Still, she supposed there was no need for him to go all out on the decor of the place when he spent only occasional nights.

She wondered what his ranch was like—and whether he'd ever invite her to go out there with him. She'd really like to see it.

"I can put on a pot of coffee or decaf," he said. "I also have a bottle of merlot."

Coffee probably was the safest bet, but she liked the idea of kicking back with him and having a glass of wine.

"The merlot sounds good," she said.

"I think so, too. Why don't you have a seat while I open the bottle."

Catherine made her way to the leather sofa and settled herself near one of the armrests, leaving room for Ray to join her. Then she watched him move about in the kitchen area as he removed a wine bottle from the pantry, two goblets from the cupboard near the sink and a corkscrew from the drawer.

He wasn't at all like the men she'd known in Manhattan, although he was pure eye candy, no matter how he was dressed. His dark hair, which was mussed from the Stetson he'd worn earlier, was a bit long and curled at his collar. She supposed some women might think it needed a trim, but she wasn't one of them. In fact, she didn't think she'd change a thing about the man.

Broad shoulders tapered down into a narrow waist, and—

Before she could continue her perusal, he turned and smiled at her.

Did he realize she'd been making an intense assessment of his lean, cowboy body, appreciating both his form and his style?

She hoped not, yet her cheeks flushed warm.

He carried the wineglasses to the sofa, then handed her one. "Here you go."

When she thanked him, he took a seat beside her.

The lamplight cast a romantic glow in the room, but it was the handsome cowboy who'd set her heart spinning, her hormones pumping and her imagination soaring.

She remembered something one of her friends had told her in Manhattan. *Once you meet another man— even if it's just a one-night stand—you'll forget all about Erik Carmichael.*

At the time, Catherine hadn't been interested in anyone else—not even to go out for a cup of coffee.

But what about Ray? Would he make the perfect transitional relationship?

She took a sip of wine, hoping to shake the thoughts that began to plague her. She couldn't very well suggest that they have an affair while she was in town, could she?

No, that would have to be Ray's idea.

"You know," he said, "I'd like to make a toast to the best hired fiancée I've ever had."

Catherine smiled, then clinked her wineglass against his. "And to the best male lead an actress ever had."

Did she dare tell him how easy her role had been? How tempted she was to stop playacting and see what developed between the two of them?

Not that she'd want to actually be engaged or marry him one day, but would making love with him be out of line? After all, if the man's kisses turned her inside out, what would a full-on sexual encounter be like?

Just the thought of it shot a warm, intoxicating buzz right through her, and she hadn't taken more than a couple of sips of wine.

"I'll sleep on the sofa tonight," he said. "You can have my room."

"That isn't fair."

"What isn't?" A boyish grin tugged at his lips, and a spark of mischief lit his eyes. "Did you want to fight me for the sofa?"

"Maybe," she said, teasing him right back.

Truth was, she'd seen his room—and the size of his bed. It was plenty big enough for both of them.

She told herself that she was just being thoughtful when she said, "There's no reason for you to sleep out here and be uncomfortable. I don't mind sharing the bed, if you don't."

The mischievous glimmer in his gaze disappeared, and something else took its place—something intense. Something masculine.

"It's not like we'd do anything other than sleep," she added by way of explanation. Yet the moment the words left her mouth, she realized she wouldn't be doing much sleeping if he were lying beside her, just an arm's reach away.

Goodness. What had she done?

She wished she could blame it on the wine, but her thoughts had taken a sexual turn the moment she'd entered his house.

When they finished their first glass, Ray poured them a second.

"Just half for me," she said. "Thank you."

After filling his glass, he walked over to the stereo and turned on the radio to a country-western station. She didn't recognize the artist or the song, but she liked the music.

"This is really nice," she said, lifting her glass and studying the deep burgundy color in the lamplight.

Yet she was talking about more than the music or the wine. She meant this moment, this man.

She was tempted to suggest something they might both regret. And with a man who was her employer. Wasn't there something unethical or inappropriate about that?

"You know," she said, "I'm going to need something to sleep in tonight. Do you have an old shirt and a pair of shorts I can use?"

"Sure." He placed his goblet on the coffee table, then strode to the bedroom.

She heard the closet door open and shut, followed by a bureau drawer.

When he returned, he held a large maroon T-shirt that sported a white Texas A and M logo on the front, as well as a pair of black boxer shorts. "How's this?"

"Perfect."

"I've also got a new toothbrush you can use," he added. "It's in the right-hand drawer in the bathroom."

"Then I'm all set." She got to her feet and took the makeshift nightwear he'd given her. "Thanks."

"You may as well take the bathroom first. You'll find clean towels hanging on the rack, in case you'd like a shower."

She offered him an appreciative smile, then headed for the bathroom, wondering what he'd say if she offered him a lot more than a smile upon her return.

Chapter Seven

While Catherine was in the bathroom, Ray walked to the window and looked out into the darkened street below. He'd been both surprised and pleased when she'd agreed to stay with him tonight. But that had nothing to do with the long drive back to the ranch and everything to do with the fact that he wanted to spend more time with her, to have her to himself for a while.

He actually looked forward to being around her, and not just because she was a pleasure to look at. He enjoyed talking to her, too. There was something very appealing about her, something alluring that went beyond sexual fascination.

Maybe it was due in part to the fact that he was safe with her. She understood that he didn't want to get romantically involved with anyone right now, so she hadn't pressed him for anything other than friendship.

Of course, if things were different, if she planned to stay in Brighton Valley—and more important, if he could be sure that the persona she'd revealed to him wasn't just part of an act—he might even ask her out on a real date, complete with soft music, candlelight, roses and wine.

But even if she was just as sincere, considerate and sweet as she appeared to be, she was going back to New York one of these days. So he'd just have to enjoy their friendship and whatever time they had left.

Now here they were, tiptoeing around all the sweet dreams and bedtime stuff.

The water shut off in the bathroom, which meant she was probably climbing from the shower and reaching for a towel, naked and wet.

That particular vision was a lot more arousing than it ought to be, but then again, the tall, leggy blonde was a beautiful woman who also seemed to have a good heart.

To top that off, he'd been serving a nearly two-year term of self-imposed celibacy, which was really starting to eat at him now—big time.

He tried to shake it off—the sexual thoughts, the arousal, but he wasn't having much luck.

Had she dried off yet? Had she slipped on his shorts and his shirt?

She'd mentioned that they could sleep together tonight, although he supposed she was only being practical. But the moment she'd suggested sharing the bed, his thoughts had taken a sexual detour.

And that's exactly where his thoughts were right now.

He could almost see her in the bathroom, wrapped in a towel and facing the fogged-up mirror. In his mind, he stood behind her, damp from the shower, too. His hands reaching for the edge of the towel, tugging it gently, removing it. Revealing that lithe dancer's body in the flesh.

He was going to drive himself crazy before she even left the bathroom.

As a soft, country love song began to play on the radio, setting off a romantic aura in the room, his libido began to battle with his good sense. In spite of his better judgment, the idea of making love with Catherine grew stronger by the heartbeat.

He probably ought to change the station and find something with a livelier beat, but he didn't make a move toward the stereo.

Instead, when the bathroom door opened, he turned to face the woman he'd envisioned naked just moments before.

Her platinum-blond hair had been swept up into a sexy twist, revealing a ballerina's neck, just begging for hot, breathy kisses.

She smiled when she spotted him, her eyes lighting up. He probably should have responded with a platonic grin of his own. Instead, he allowed his gaze to sweep over her, amazed by those long, shapely legs that could wrap around a man and make him cry uncle. Or aunt. Or whatever else she had in mind.

"It's a little steamy in there," she said.

Hell, it was even steamier out *here*. And while he had no business making any kind of sexual innuendo, he couldn't help speaking his mind. "Seeing you like that…" His gaze sketched over her again, making it difficult to continue without acting upon his arousal.

"I can change into something else," she said, glancing down at the shirt she wore, "if you'd be more comfortable. Or…"

Or *what?* Was she going to suggest that they let nature take its course this evening?

Sure, why not? he wanted to say.

She didn't continue the open-ended option, but the way she was looking at him—which had to be the same way he was looking at her—didn't leave a whole lot of doubt that her thoughts had taken a sexual turn, too. But hey, why shouldn't they?

He could throw out the idea, he supposed, laying it on the table—or wherever else they might end up. But what would he do if she told him it wasn't in her job description?

Then again, he might kick himself later for letting a once-in-a-lifetime opportunity slip through his hands.

"How long has it been for you?" he asked, stepping out on a limb that swayed under the weight of the question.

"Since I've had sex?" She gave a little shrug. "Quite a while. How about you?"

Had he actually been celibate for two long years?

After he and his ex had split, it had seemed like a good way to avoid getting caught in another bad relationship before he had time to get over the last one. But now?

He couldn't imagine going without sex for a minute longer.

They stood like that for a moment—too far away from each other to touch, yet connected in a way he hadn't expected.

"I know that a short-term affair wasn't part of our bargain," she said, "but I wouldn't be opposed to it."

At that, his pulse rate shot through the roof, and his mouth went dry, then wet. Before meeting Catherine, he hadn't really missed sex all that much. Not that he'd planned to give it up for good.

But now? When the opportunity of a lifetime was knocking?

He took a step forward, then another. "I wouldn't be opposed to it, either."

"It might actually help us both move along in the healing process," she said.

There was no doubt about that. Just the thought of taking Catherine in his arms had his heart spinning—and all in one piece—strong, vibrant, whole.

"We've definitely got chemistry," he said as they met in the middle of the room.

"That's true. If the kisses we shared were any indication of how good it would be between us…"

He finished the thought for her. "Then making love is going to be off the charts."

She nodded.

Still, he didn't make a move.

And neither did she.

When she bit down on her bottom lip, he wondered if it was a shy reaction to what was going on between them or if it was… No, it wasn't part of her act. Neither of them were playing a role right now. This—whatever *this* was—had to be real.

For a while, he'd wondered where fantasy ended and reality began when it came to his feelings for her. But when push came to shove, he had to admit that he'd quit playacting about the time of their very first kiss.

In fact, he'd even become intrigued by the idea of dating her and… What? Pursuing her?

Maybe so—at least, that was his game plan tonight.

When Ray opened his arms and Catherine stepped into his embrace, he relished her clean, fresh-from-the-shower scent, as well as the feel of her soft breasts pressed against his chest.

He realized she must be entertaining a similar game plan because she wrapped her arms around his neck and drew his lips to hers. As their tongues met, their kiss exploded with passion, with heat.

She tasted of peppermint, of sunshine and dreams, and he couldn't get enough of her. His hands sought, stroked and explored every uncovered inch of her, but still he wanted more, needed more. He reached for the hemline of her T-shirt, lifting the fabric, revealing her bare waist, her taut belly, her perfect curves….

When his hand reached her breasts, he cupped the soft mounds, caressed them. As his thumb skimmed across her nipple, her breath caught.

Damn. He couldn't believe his good fortune. They were actually going through with this, and he couldn't be happier—no matter what tomorrow brought. And by the way Catherine was responding to his touch, to his kiss, he had a feeling she felt the very same way.

* * *

Caught up in an amazing swirl of heat and desire, Catherine leaned into the rugged cowboy and gripped his shoulders as if she might collapse if she hadn't. And who knew? Maybe she would have.

Never had she wanted a man so badly, so desperately. If she didn't know better, she'd swear that they'd been made for each other—their bodies, their hearts, their souls.

She kissed him back for all she was worth, wanting him, wanting this.

There might be a hundred reasons they shouldn't allow themselves to get carried away tonight, but tell that to her raging hormones. Right now, all she wanted to do was let him work his cowboy magic on her and take her someplace she'd never been.

As the kiss ended, they clung to each other, their breaths ragged, their hearts pounding.

"Let's take this to the bedroom," Ray whispered against her cheek.

She didn't trust herself to speak, so she slipped her hand in his and allowed him to take her anywhere he wanted to go.

They padded across the hardwood floor, and moments later, when they reached the bed, he took her in his arms again and kissed her until her thoughts spun out of control, until nothing else mattered other than this man and this night.

His hands slid along the curves of her back, then he pulled her hips forward, against his erection. She arched forward, showing him her need, as well as her willingness to make love to him.

When she thought she'd melt into a puddle if they didn't climb into bed and finish what they'd started, she ended the kiss, then she removed the T-shirt he'd loaned her. As she let the garment drop to the floor, she stood before him in nothing but the boxers he'd loaned her.

His gaze caressed her as intimately as his hands had done just seconds earlier. "You're beautiful, Catherine."

Her only response was to reach for his belt buckle and to begin removing his clothing, too. She needed to feel his bare skin against hers, and she couldn't wait another minute.

Together, they removed his shirt, and she marveled at his broad chest, his six-pack abs.

Catherine wasn't a novice at lovemaking. She'd had lovers before—two, in fact. But neither of those men had been built as strong and sturdy as Ray, whose muscles were a result of both genetics and hard work.

"You're beautiful, too," she said.

After they'd drawn back the spread and slipped into bed, Ray showed her how a cowboy loved a lady, creating a memory she'd never forget.

They moved together in rhythm that built until they reached a breath-stealing peak. As she cried out with her release, he let go, too, climaxing in a burst of fireworks and spinning stars.

Never had she felt such passion or experienced such an earth-shattering orgasm.

As she lay in Ray's arms, relishing the stunning afterglow, a sated smile stretched across her face. She'd expected their lovemaking to be good, but she'd never imagined it would be like this.

She tried to tell herself that it was merely a physical act, that there wasn't anything emotional going on. Making love with Ray had been a great way to completely shake any lingering disillusionment she'd had after her breakup with Erik. Yet she found herself wading through a rush of emotions she hadn't expected.

As she pondered those budding feelings, Ray stiffened, then rolled to the side.

Was something wrong?

"I, uh…hate to put a damper on things," he said, propping himself up on an elbow and casting a shadow over the sweet afterglow she'd thought they'd both been enjoying.

Her stomach knotted, and disappointment flared. Just moments ago, everything had seemed right—perfect, if not promising. Was he regretting what they'd done?

The possibility sent her tender emotions into a tailspin, making her question the value she'd placed on their lovemaking. As her mind scampered to make sense of it all—not only the budding emotion their joining had stirred within her, but also her agreement to enter into a fake engagement in the first place. What had she been thinking?

Determined to protect herself, she decided to downplay their joining and her unexpected emotional reaction to it.

"It was just a physical act," she said, "something we both needed."

"Yes, I know." He brushed a strand of hair from her brow in a sweet and gentle manner, yet the look on his face remained serious, sending her a mixed message.

"This doesn't mean we have to change our employment agreement," she said, taking a guess as to what might be bothering him. "And don't worry. I'm not going to ask for any kind of commitment or chase after you like some of the local women have done."

"I know that." While his expression seemed to soften, his demeanor remained tense, maybe even defensive.

"Then what's bothering you?" she asked.

"You don't know?"

No, she didn't. That's why she'd assumed that he was regretting what they'd done. And why she'd tried to assuage whatever worry he might have.

As he slowly shook his head and clicked his tongue, she braced herself for the worst.

"We didn't use any protection," he said.

Oh, no. He was right. They hadn't.

"And it's not like me to be irresponsible."

It wasn't like her to neglect something important like that, either. But apparently, they'd gotten so carried away with the passion that they'd lost their heads.

"You might have gotten pregnant," he added. "And that's a complication neither of us needs right now."

She appreciated his concern, but at least she could put his worries about that to rest. "It's not the right time of the month for me to conceive. And even if it were, it isn't likely. I've been told my chances of having a baby are slim."

"I'm sorry to hear that."

She was sorry, too, but she'd come to accept it. "It was depressing to hear that news when the doctor told me, but I'm okay with it now. Dan and Eva's twins have adopted me as their auntie, so I'm glad to be a part of their lives."

The conversation was getting entirely too heavy and too sad to deal with after such an amazing bout of lovemaking. And while Ray might have said that he hadn't wanted to put a damper on things, he'd done just that.

She rolled slightly, moving away from him. Then she slipped out of his arms, climbed from bed and headed for the bathroom.

"Are you okay?" he asked.

She turned, glanced over her shoulder and offered him her brightest smile. "Of course."

But she *wasn't* okay. She was struggling with rejection, disappointment and the sudden reminder that she'd never have a baby of her own. Not that she'd expected to have one with Ray, but at least for a moment or two while making love, she'd entertained the brief fantasy of having it all someday: a husband and children, a home in the suburbs. Yet for some reason, and without any warning, that dream fell apart before it could even begin.

She had to find some solid ground on which to stand and some time to ponder what they'd just done, what she'd briefly imagined it to be and what she would do about it now.

When she'd kissed him, when she'd agreed to make love, she'd only thought of it as a sexual act. Yet thanks to the chemistry between them, it had been even better than she'd anticipated. Amazing, actually. And it had seemed to be a whole lot more than physical.

Surely, she'd only imagined the emotional side of it—at least, on her part. So until she could sort through it all and figure out a way out of it, she needed to be alone for a while.

If that darn pickup wasn't having engine trouble, she'd tell Ray that she was driving back to the ranch tonight. But as it was, she was stuck here until morning.

After their lovemaking last night, Catherine had stayed in the bathroom for what had seemed like hours, although it was probably only a matter of minutes. She hadn't seemed the least bit concerned about pregnancy, which should have made Ray feel better. But for some reason, it hadn't helped at all. He'd still been uneasy about the whole thing.

Not that he regretted making love with her. The time spent in her arms had been incredible, a real fantasy come true. But now that the new day had dawned, so had reality.

A relationship between the two of them, which had seemed so feasible in the heat of the moment, was no longer viable. The possibility had dissipated the moment Catherine had returned to the bedroom, only to curl up on her side of the mattress, rather than cuddle with him.

Now, as he lay stretched out on the bed, trying to set aside the uneasiness that had niggled at him all through the night, he tried to focus on the memory of their lovemaking. Of course, any sexual encounter would have been great after a two-year dry spell.

Or would it?

When he tried to imagine being in bed with another woman, each time he gazed into the fantasy woman's eyes, he saw Catherine smiling back at him, urging him on.

He told himself that was because the memory of their lovemaking was so fresh in his mind, so *real*. In that one, amazing moment, when the two of them had become one, climaxing at the same time, he'd wanted to hold on to her and never let her go. He'd also been tempted to spill his heart and soul to her—if he'd actually thought that what he'd been feeling for her had been real. But as his heart rate and his breathing slowed to a normal pace, he'd realized that he'd neglected to use a condom, that he hadn't even had the foresight to purchase any ahead of time. And the irresponsibility left him completely unbalanced.

He appreciated the fact that pregnancy wasn't an issue, but he had other concerns, too. Like becoming emotionally attached to a woman who wouldn't be in Brighton Valley forever.

Besides, just because sex between a couple was absolutely incredible, especially the very first time, didn't mean that they'd be compatible.

When the bathroom door clicked open, and Catherine walked out wearing the clothes she'd worn to the community barbecue last night, she cast a friendly smile his way. Yet they really weren't friends at this point. In fact, he wasn't sure what they were to each other. He supposed they were lovers, but would that be true if this was just a one-night thing?

He had no idea. Still, he sat up in bed, determined to face the uncertainty of the day.

"Would you like to eat breakfast here or at Caroline's Diner?" he asked.

"If you don't mind, I'd really like to get back to the ranch. I promised Eva I'd help her with the kids this morning."

He wished he could say he was relieved, yet for some reason, he hated to see her go, which made no sense.

Nevertheless, he threw off the covers and climbed out of bed. "No problem. I'll take a quick shower, then I'll drive you back to the ranch."

"Thanks."

Again she smiled.

And again, he sensed there was something missing in her expression.

He'd never seen her like this—wrapped up in some kind of invisible armor, her thoughts a million miles away.

She'd withdrawn last night, right after their climax. Had she been truthful when she'd told him not to worry about pregnancy?

Or was she angry that he hadn't been more responsible?

No, she couldn't be mad about that. She should have thought about the consequences of unprotected sex, too.

Was she kicking herself for letting it happen? He

supposed he wouldn't know unless he addressed the issue.

"Is everything okay?" he asked.

"Yes, it's fine." She crossed the room and placed a kiss on his cheek as if trying to convince him, yet failing miserably.

Something still wasn't right.

"Are you sorry about what we did last night?" he asked.

"No, not at all." She offered him another smile he couldn't trust. "How about you?"

"I'm not the least bit sorry." Okay, so that wasn't entirely true. He wasn't sorry about having sex—and he doubted that he ever would be. His only real regret stemmed from her mood change and the distance between them.

As Ray went into the bathroom and shut the door, he tried to rehash everything that had gone on the night before so he could figure out what went wrong—and *when*.

The lovemaking itself seemed perfect.

When he'd rolled to the side and gazed at her, she'd been wearing a serene smile—a *real* one. And that proved that they'd shared the same pleasure.

It was only after she'd returned from the bathroom that things had grown a little…chilly.

Shouldn't he be happy that she wasn't putting any pressure on him, especially when she'd be moving back to New York soon?

Or had he begun to fall in love with an actress? A woman who pretended to be someone else?

By the time he got out of the shower, he wasn't any closer to having an answer than he'd been last night.

Even after he'd dried off and gotten dressed, he still wasn't sure what was going on between them— or how he ought to feel about it. But there was one thing he did know. He was in danger of falling in love with a woman who might not exist.

When he entered the living area, Catherine was seated on the sofa, waiting for him.

"You know," he said, as he grabbed his keys from the dinette table, "I was thinking. We've done a good job convincing everyone in town that I'm engaged. And after that announcement at the barbecue last night, people will know I'm off-limits. We probably don't need to be seen together constantly."

"You're probably right." She got to her feet. "Just give me a call at the ranch if you need me again."

For what? Another date to a community event he had to attend. Or for another night of lovemaking?

Damn. It almost sounded as if she was ending it all—their employment, their friendship, their… What? Their star-crossed affair?

An ache burrowed deep in his chest, and he wished that he could roll back the clock twelve hours and start over. But it was too late to backpedal now.

"There's not much going on for another week," he said, "but I'm sure I'll need you again."

"No problem. Just let me know when."

He locked up his apartment, then followed her down the stairwell.

"How much longer do you plan to be in town?" he asked.

"I'm not entirely sure. But probably as long as you might need me."

For a moment, he was tempted to say that he'd like for her to extend her visit, that he had a feeling he would need her for a long, long time. But he couldn't say that. Instead, he thanked her for all she'd done to help him.

"And I'd also like to thank you for…last night. It was amazing. Maybe we can do it again sometime. But if not, that's okay, too."

"I feel the same way."

Did she?

He certainly hoped they weren't on the same page, because he hated not having a game plan. And he had no idea where to go from here.

Chapter Eight

The drive back to the Walker ranch was fairly quiet, other than the sound of the music playing softly on the car radio.

Catherine hoped that she'd put Ray's worries to rest, although she wished she could say the same for herself. What had happened last night?

If she didn't know better, she'd think that she might actually fall for Ray—if she wasn't careful.

And if that was the case, then it really was for the best that they slow down their time spent together. Ray had made it more than clear that he didn't have any interest in striking up a romance—with *anyone*.

Besides, she had a life in New York. Getting involved with the Brighton Valley mayor wasn't a good idea. And if she let her feelings get in the way, their relationship—or whatever it was—could end in disappointment or heartbreak. And heaven knew she didn't need to risk having something like that happen.

When they arrived at the ranch, Ray kept the engine running.

"I have a meeting in Wexler with a couple of investors at noon," he said. "And while I'm in the area, I thought it would be a good idea if I talked to my foreman first. So, if you don't mind, I'm just going to drop you off. Can you tell Dan and Eva I said hello?"

"Of course."

His gaze zeroed in on hers, reaching out in a way that gripped her heart and nearly squeezed the beat right out of it.

"One more thing," he said.

She stiffened, and her breathing slowed to a near stop as she readied herself for whatever he had to say.

"Thanks again for last night. It was *amazing. You* were amazing. And it was both a gift and a memory I'll cherish."

Emotion balled up in her throat, making it difficult to speak. Yet, somehow, she found her voice and mustered a smile. "I thought it was special, too. And, for the record, I'm not sorry about it." At least, she didn't regret making love with him. It was the unexpected emotional fallout that had her scampering to make sense of it all.

"I'll give you a call in a day or two," he said.

"Sounds good." She lifted her hand in a wave, then watched him back up his SUV, as if he was backing out of her life forever.

She'd told him that she wasn't sorry, and in a sense,

that was true. But now that she'd opened up to him, now that they'd shared a physical intimacy as well, she had to admit that she grieved for what might have developed between them. Because, if truth be told, she would have been tempted to remain in Brighton Valley indefinitely if he'd given her any reason to think that he'd wanted her to.

And how crazy was that? Her life and her career were in Manhattan. Giving up everything she'd ever wanted, everything she'd achieved, for a man was unthinkable. Yet the thought had crossed her mind just the same.

Catherine turned and headed for the ranch house. After climbing the steps and crossing the porch, she opened the front door and entered the living room, where Kaylee and a little red-haired girl sat beside a pink-and-chrome child's karaoke machine, five or six dolls surrounding them.

Upon seeing Catherine, Kaylee brightened. "You're home!"

She smiled, glad that she'd been missed. But at this point in time, she wasn't really sure where "home" was. Her apartment in Greenwich Village had been sublet for six more weeks, so she couldn't even fly back to New York if she wanted to. Still, she said to the child she thought of as a daughter, "Yes, sweetie. I'm home."

She watched the two girls set the dolls in a semi-circle. "What are you doing, Kaylee-bug?"

"Me and my new friend, Shauna, are making a Broadway show for our dolls, just like you do. And after we practice, we're going to invite you and our moms to watch it. Well, not her mom. But her..." Kaylee turned to the red-haired girl. "Who is she again?"

"She's my foster mom, I guess." Shauna, a tall, gangly child who appeared to be a year or so older than Kaylee, gave a little shrug. "Her name is Jane Morrison. And she's a lot nicer than the last one I had before."

Catherine's heart went out to the girl, with big green eyes haunted by sadness.

In an effort to let Shauna know that her situation wasn't all that unusual, Catherine said, "I'm kind of like Kaylee's foster mom, too."

"Yeah," Kaylee said. "When my mommy died, me and my brother lived with Catherine. Then we moved to the ranch with my Uncle Dan and Aunt Eva. But now that we're adopted, they're our dad and mom."

"Sometimes life gets complicated," Catherine said to the child, yet the reality of the words echoed in her mind, reminding her of Ray and of the awkward situation she'd created for herself.

"Shauna goes to my church," Kaylee added. "And on Monday, she gets to go to my school. I'm going to ask Mrs. Parker, the principal, to let her be in my class."

"It's nice to meet you," Catherine said. "And I'm glad you'll have at least one friend when Monday comes around."

"That's why Mrs. Morrison brought her to our house today," Kaylee said. "She's already gone to about a hundred different schools."

"Only four," Shauna corrected. "But that's okay. I'm used to being a new kid."

Catherine doubted anyone ever got used to being moved around that much or placed in new households, but she let the subject drop and asked, "Where's your mom, Kaylee?"

"She's in the kitchen."

Catherine set her purse on the bottom step of the stairway, planning to carry it up later. Then she made her way through the house, eager to find Eva and seek some advice—that is, if she had the courage to tell her what she'd done.

When she entered the kitchen, she spotted her friend standing at the sink, chopping vegetables to add to the Crock-Pot on the counter.

"Need any help?" Catherine asked.

Eva turned and smiled. "Thanks, but I've got it under control. How was the barbecue?"

"It was fun. The food was great, the music, too. And I really enjoyed the people I met."

"I'm sorry we missed it, but I couldn't take Kevin after he twisted his ankle."

"Where is he?"

"Dan took him to the Urgent Care in town to have an X-ray. We really don't think he fractured it, but it was still swollen and sore this morning. So we wanted to get a doctor's opinion—and to make sure he didn't have any serious tissue damage."

"I'm sorry I wasn't here earlier," Catherine said. "I could have watched the kids for you. Then you both could have taken him to the doctor."

"No, Dan can handle it. Besides, Kaylee has a friend over today, and it was important that I stayed home for that."

Catherine took a seat at the table. As she did so, she realized that the house was unusually quiet. "Where are the little ones?"

"Uncle Pete took them on a nature walk. Then he's going to put on a cartoon movie at his house and feed them lunch. I wanted Kaylee and Shauna to have some time alone so they could get to know each other better."

"Kaylee introduced me to her. She seems like a nice little girl, but I feel sorry for her."

"You don't know the half of it," Eva said, her voice lowered. "Her mother died when she was just a toddler. And somehow, she ended up with the stepfather. When he went to prison, she was placed in foster care. From what I understand, her maternal grandmother finally got custody, only to be diagnosed with terminal cancer a few months later. The poor kid has really been through a lot."

"I'm glad Kaylee is reaching out to her. How did you meet her?"

"Jane Morrison, one of the women in our church, is her new foster parent. And she asked if we could help with the transition." Eva turned back to her work long enough to put the veggies into the Crock-Pot, then she washed her hands at the sink. "How about a cup of herbal tea? I just put on a pot of water to heat."

"Sounds good."

Eva carried the sugar bowl, spoons and a variety of tea bags she kept in a small wicker basket to the table. Then she filled two cups with hot water, setting one in front of Catherine. She'd no sooner taken a seat when she asked, "What's the matter?"

"Nothing." Catherine opened a packet of Earl Grey, then dropped the tea bag into her cup of water. "Why?"

"I don't know. You look a little tired, I guess."

It was, Catherine decided, a perfect opening to tell Eva why she felt so uneasy, what she and Ray had done. But she wasn't sure if she was ready to admit to all of that—or if she'd ever be ready. So she said, "I guess I'm just a little tired. I didn't get much sleep last night."

"Sometimes that happens when you sleep in an unfamiliar bed."

"Yes, I'm sure that's it." Catherine glanced down at the steeping tea bag, wishing the leaves were loose instead of contained, wishing she could empty the cup and read her future.

"Uh-oh," Eva said.

Catherine glanced up at her friend, and as their gazes met, Eva cocked her head to the side as if she'd read Catherine's mind.

"I sense that something's either *very* right," Eva said, "or *very* wrong."

At first, Catherine assumed she was talking about the children, but when she caught the knowing look in Eva's eyes, she realized the conversation had taken a personal turn.

"What do you mean?" she asked.

"You and Ray might be faking an engagement, but you look good together. And you're both as nice as can be. If you lived in town, or had plans to stay, I'd probably encourage you to consider him as a romantic possibility."

"But I *don't* plan to stay in town," Catherine said, more determined to leave now than ever.

"I know." Eva took a sip of tea, and a smile tugged across her lips. "The two of you would make a great couple. And since you're both nursing broken hearts, it seems natural that one or the other or both of you would find the other attractive. And that in itself might be the cause for a restless night."

Yes, and so would the emotional aftereffects of great sex, especially when a romantic future didn't look the least bit promising.

Before Catherine was forced to either lie or to admit more than she was willing to share, Kaylee came bounding into the kitchen. "It's time for the show. Will you please come and watch us?"

"I wouldn't miss it for the world." Eva picked up her cup and looked at Catherine. "Do you mind bringing your tea into the living room? They've been practicing all morning."

"No, not at all." Catherine picked up her cup and saucer, then followed Eva and Kaylee back to the living room.

"There's going to be a talent show in our school cafeteria," Kaylee told Catherine. "And me and Shauna are going to be in it. We're going to sing and dance, just like you and my mommy."

Shauna kind of scrunched up her face. "It's Kaylee's idea. She wants me to be the singer, and she's going to dance."

"There's a talent show at the kids' school?" Catherine asked Eva. Could it be the same one she'd heard about while attending the hospital benefit with Ray? The one Dr. Ramirez had suggested she take part in?

"The Brighton Valley Junior Women's Club is sponsoring it," Eva explained. "There's been a lot of talk about building a center for the arts on the new side of town, and they'd wanted a fundraiser. They're even encouraging the school children who sing, dance or play an instrument to participate."

"That's really nice." Catherine would have loved getting involved in a community event like that when she'd been a girl.

"And Catherine," Kaylee said, "you can be in it, too. You could sing that song about the raindrops on roses, the one you used to sing to me and Kevin."

Catherine smiled, remembering the days when she lived with the twins. "You're talking about 'My Favorite Things' from *The Sound of Music*."

"Yes, that's the one," Kaylee said. "Will you sing it at our school? And can you wear a beautiful costume like the ones you have in New York?"

Kaylee had been only five when her mother died, but she still remembered the times Jennifer and Catherine would take her backstage to see the costumes and props. One set in particular had been a pirate ship, and Kevin had loved the tour one of the stagehands had given him. But Kaylee had especially enjoyed seeing some of the gowns up close.

"It would be really nice if you participated," Eva added, "especially since you're 'engaged' to the mayor. I'm sure he'd be pleased if you did."

Catherine wasn't sure what would please Ray these days, although she suspected he'd like the idea. And she missed performing for an audience—no matter what the size. But she didn't want to upstage any of the local talent—not when she was a professional.

"I don't mind getting involved with the talent show," Catherine said, "but I don't think it's a good idea if I compete with any of the local townspeople."

"I understand," Eva said. "It might not be fair to everyone involved. But maybe you could perform at the end of the evening. Or what if the grand prize was a voice or dance lesson from you?"

"It would have to be up to the committee heading up the event," Catherine said, "but I'm willing to do anything I can to help out."

"What about *us?*" Kaylee said. "You can give lessons to me and Shauna so we can be the winners."

"You'll always be a winner in my heart," Catherine said. "And I'd love to give you two a few pointers."

The girls clapped their hands with glee, then turned on the karaoke machine. Within minutes, they put on a darling show.

Shauna, who belted out a Hannah Montana/Miley Cyrus hit, had a natural talent that nearly knocked Catherine off her chair. On the other hand, Kaylee, bless her heart, hadn't inherited her mother's dancing ability.

Then again, maybe she just needed a few pointers. Either way, the kid had heart. And their performance brought maternal tears to Catherine's eyes.

When the "show" ended, the women broke into applause, praising both girls.

"I'll tell you what," Catherine said as she swiped

at her watery eyes with her fingers. "I'd be happy to coach you girls for the community talent show."

Kaylee squealed in delight, while Shauna smiled.

"And I'll make the costumes," Eva added as she placed her hand on the red-haired girl's shoulder. "I'm also going to ask Shauna's foster mom to help me. This is going to be so much fun."

She was right. Catherine was going to enjoy helping the girls. She was also looking forward to having something to do over the next few weeks that would help to keep her mind not only off Ray, but off the mess she might have made out of their budding friendship.

After dropping Catherine off at the Walkers' place, Ray had driven twenty minutes to his own ranch to talk to Mark Halstead, his foreman. He could have used his cell phone rather than make the trip in person, but he'd needed to get some perspective, and there was no better way to do that than to step onto the old family homestead, to breathe in the country air, to see the cattle grazing in the pastures.

The bluebonnets his mother had loved dotted the hillsides these days, and while seeing them wasn't the same as entering her kitchen and finding her baking homemade cinnamon rolls as a treat, it was the best he could do.

He'd hoped that once Catherine had gotten out of his Escalade, he'd be able to sort through what had happened, and then decide what he wanted to do about it—if anything.

All morning long, he'd been beating himself up,

although he wasn't sure why. He wasn't sorry they'd had sex, although it had definitely changed things between them. And he had no idea if that change had been good or not.

For one thing, he'd come pretty damn close to falling for Catherine Loza, another city girl who'd never want to be a rancher's wife. And to make matters worse, she would be leaving soon—and taking a part of his heart with him, if he was fool enough to offer it to her.

You'd think that after all the hell his ex-wife had put him through, he'd be fighting to remain single and unattached for the rest of his life. Not that he would ever broach the idea of a commitment with Catherine.

Besides, she'd said it herself. *It was just a physical act, something we both needed.*

And she'd certainly been right about that. He'd needed the release more than he'd realized. Maybe he'd needed the intimacy, too. He'd come from a very small but close family who'd been both loving and supportive. But as each family member had died, one after the other, he'd slowly lost parts of his connection to someone who'd loved him unconditionally.

He'd actually hoped that Heather would have stepped up to the plate in that respect, but whatever connection they'd had began to fray the day she'd moved in with him. And that was fine with him. He'd learned to get by without those family ties.

Besides, he had good friends who'd been supportive, like Dan Walker and Shane Hollister.

Yet in just a few days, he'd begun to feel that bond and the sense of kinship again—*with Catherine,* as strange as that might seem. Their whole relationship, whether they were friends or lovers, had been based upon a lie. So how could he place any value on whatever feelings he might be having for her, especially when he had no idea how much—if any—of the real Catherine she'd actually revealed to him. She could be putting on one hell of a show, and he wouldn't know the difference.

Still, he couldn't quite bring himself to let her go. It might be foolishness on his part—or a bad case of lust—but he didn't like the idea of ending her employment just yet. If he did, he'd have to explain their breakup to everyone in town.

Okay, so that's the excuse he was making to continue their charade—and he hadn't even reached the family homestead yet or breathed the country air that seemed to clear his mind.

As he neared the feed lot, which was only five miles from the long, graveled driveway that led to his ranch, he began to realize that he had another reason for maintaining the phony fiancée plan, and it wasn't nearly as practical.

Or maybe it was. He'd been yearning for something elusive, something he seemed to have temporarily found with Catherine.

Call him a fool, but after allowing them both some time to think, some time to put things into perspective, he was going to ask her to attend another function with him.

So what was next on his calendar?

The only thing he could think of was that birthday

dinner at the American Legion Hall to honor Ernie Tucker.

Ernie, who'd been the first sheriff in Brighton Valley, was going to be one hundred years old on the fourteenth of the month. So the town had planned to have festivities all weekend long, beginning with the fancy dinner. There was going to be a parade down Main Street on Saturday, and finally, on Sunday morning, the Brighton Valley Community Church would have an ice cream social in his honor.

If you asked Ray, it seemed a bit much. Poor old Ernie was going to be plumb worn out from celebrating come Monday. But not many folks could claim to reach a milestone birthday like that, especially when they were still spry and sharp as a tack.

So now he had a good reason to call Catherine and set up another date—so to speak.

Why was it that he couldn't wait to distance himself from her just moments ago, yet now he was thinking about seeing her again?

He wasn't going to ponder the answer to that, but attending a birthday celebration with her seemed safe enough.

When he spotted the three oak trees that grew near the county road, marking the property line at the southernmost part of his ranch, he imagined being with her on the night of Ernie's dinner party, walking down the quiet city street, feeling the heat of her touch as his hand reached for hers.

And as he let the fantasy take wing, he imagined taking her back to his apartment, this time with a game plan that included a night's supply of condoms, a room full of candles and anything else he could think of to create the perfect romantic setting.

It was a risky thing to do, he supposed, especially since any kind of a relationship between them would last as long as an icicle in hell.

But then, tell that to his libido.

Every day that following week, after Kaylee and Shauna got out of school, Catherine worked with them on their dance steps, as well as on the song they planned to perform for the talent show. Eva had insisted that the other children stay out of the way so the girls could practice without interruption. And while there were a few complaints from the younger twins, they forgot their disappointment as soon as Eva suggested a new outdoor activity to keep them occupied.

As a result, Kaylee and Shauna worked hard. It didn't take Catherine long to realize they stood a chance to win, especially if the competition was divided into age groups.

"Shauna," she said, "I think it's time you tried to sing without using the karaoke screen."

"I don't know about that." The shy, gangly girl bit down on her bottom lip. "I'm not sure I can do it without the words."

Catherine smiled. "Actually, you haven't been relying on the screen that much anyway. Why don't you give it a try and see how it goes?"

"O-kay."

Before Catherine could start the music, her cell phone rang. She would have ignored the call completely, but it might be Ray. And she...

Well, they hadn't seen each other since last Saturday, although things seemed to be okay both times they'd talked on the phone. So she was eager to…

What? Hear his voice?

She clicked her tongue as she glanced at the lighted display, and when she recognized his number, her heart stopped momentarily, then spun in a perfect pirouette.

You'd think she'd been waiting for days to hear from him. And, well…okay, she *had*.

"Excuse me, girls. I need to take this call." As she prepared to answer, she walked out of the living room and onto the porch, telling herself he probably had something work-related to say and nothing that would require her to seek privacy. But she still didn't want an audience, just in case.

Once she was out of earshot, she said, "Hello."

"Hey, it's me." They were just three little words—not even three that held any real importance, yet the deep timbre of his voice shot a thrill clean through her.

"Hey, yourself," she responded.

"Am I bothering you?"

"No, not at all."

"Good. I called to ask if you were available to attend a few functions with me next weekend."

Not until then? She shook off a tinge of disappointment. "Sure, what's up?"

"There's a birthday party at the American Legion Hall on Friday night for Ernie Tucker, one of Brighton Valley's oldest residents. There's also a parade in his honor on Saturday and an ice-cream social at the community church after services on Sunday. Can you attend all of them with me?"

She didn't see any reason why not.

"You're welcome to stay with me in town," he added, "if you'd like to."

Her heart thumped and bumped around in her chest like the worn-out rods and pistons in the ranch pickup she'd driven into town last week. The one that hadn't been safe for her to drive home.

You're welcome to stay with me in town...if you'd like to.

Oh, she'd like to all right. Her thoughts drifted to the night she and Ray had slept together, and she was sorely tempted to agree. At least her body was eager. But her heart and mind were telling her to slow down and give it some careful thought.

Was he actually suggesting that she spend three days and two nights with him in his apartment in town?

"We can always figure something else out," he added. "I can take you home between the events—or you can drive yourself. It's really up to you."

"Let's take one day at a time."

At least that would give her time to think things through.

"By the way," she said, "what's the dress code on Friday night?"

"Whatever you're comfortable wearing. Some people will be casual, while others might get dressed up. I'll probably wear a sport jacket."

"And for the parade?" she asked.

"Slacks, I guess. Or maybe jeans, if you'd prefer. Nothing fancy."

"How about the ice-cream social?"

"Well, that's casual, too. But I suspect some people will have on their church clothes." He paused for a moment, as though wanting to say something else.

When it became apparent that he had nothing more to add, she said, "I'll be glad to go with you. Why don't I meet you in town on Friday evening?"

"You mean at my apartment, right?"

She wasn't sure what she meant. "Okay, I'll meet you there. We can talk about the sleeping arrangements later."

He paused a beat. "Fair enough."

There was so much left unsaid that the silence filled the line until it grew too heavy to ignore. But instead of mentioning the chasm their lovemaking had created between them, she told him goodbye and promised that they'd talk again—soon.

Yet thoughts about the future followed her back to the living room, where the girls had continued to practice without her.

She'd no more than taken a seat when her cell phone rang again. She glanced at the display, thinking Ray might have forgotten to tell her something, but she recognized Zoe Grimwood's number.

"I'm so sorry," she told the girls. "But I need to take this call, too."

As Catherine returned to the patio, eager to hear what was going on in Manhattan, she greeted her friend.

"Guess what?" Zoe said. "Word is out that Paul

De Santos has managed to pull things together financially. And he's going to start casting parts for *Dancing the Night Away*."

That was the show Erik had been producing when he'd left town, taking several large investments with him.

"I saw the script," Zoe added. "And the lead would be perfect for you."

Erik had said the same thing—before he'd talked Catherine into investing fifty thousand dollars of her own money into the project. The man she'd trusted had burned her in many ways when he'd left. The most difficult, of course, had been facing the irate investors and telling them she had no answers for any of their questions.

"I'm not sure how Paul would feel about me auditioning for any of the parts," Catherine said. "He probably blames me. Erik left him holding the bag. He had to deal with the investors who'd lost their money and try to make things right."

"Paul can't hold you responsible," Zoe said. "You invested in the project, too."

Still, Catherine had been dating Erik, so she should have been able to see through him. If Paul considered her guilty by association, she'd never land the part. So, no matter how badly she wanted it, why should she even audition?

"I'll have to think about it," she said.

"Why? That part was made for you. And Paul has to know it."

She was certainly tempted. If she went back to New York and landed a role in the very musical Erik had been trying to produce, it might vindicate her in the eyes of everyone she'd ever known or worked with on Broadway.

Catherine crossed the porch and peered through the window, into the living room, where the girls continued to practice their dance steps.

"I've got a commitment here for the next couple of weeks," Catherine said. "I can't come immediately."

She also had a commitment to Ray, the job he'd asked her to do. And then there was their budding romance or whatever they'd been tiptoeing around.

Tiptoeing around? That sounded as if they were both considering some kind of relationship, when she didn't know *what* either of them were actually thinking, let alone feeling.

She slowly shook her head. She'd better get the stars out of her eyes, or she could end up brokenhearted again. Ray had made it clear that he didn't want to date anyone. Otherwise, he wouldn't have hired her to keep the women at bay.

So what made her think he'd be interested in her—other than the fact that she was safe and would be leaving soon?

And worse, what if she was wrong? What if he actually considered striking up a romance with her? And what if she were foolish enough to go along with it?

She might end up married to the guy—and stuck in a small town forever.

"How's your knee?" Zoe asked.

When Catherine had been in New York, she'd been having a little trouble with it. She'd considered seeing a specialist, but the down time had really helped. "It's a lot better than it was—in fact, I think it's completely healed, although it's still a little stiff."

And that reminded her. If she was going to return to Broadway, she'd have to start working out again. She'd also have to lose a couple of pounds.

"Okay," she told Zoe. "I'll do it. Once I have my flight scheduled, I'll give you a call."

At that moment, Kaylee ran out to the patio and tugged at Catherine's sleeve. Then she pointed toward the living room, where Shauna was belting out the song.

"She's not looking at the screen," Kaylee whispered, her eyes bright. "She's doing it, just like Hannah Montana!"

Catherine smiled at the child she thought of as a daughter and gave her a wink, then returned to her telephone conversation with Zoe. "I can return in a little over two weeks, but I won't have access to my apartment for another three. Will you let me stay with you for a while?"

"Absolutely."

"Okay, then. It's all set."

As she ended the call, she told herself it was time to go home. It was the right thing to do.

The *only* thing.

Chapter Nine

On Friday night, twenty minutes before the birthday party was scheduled to start, Catherine arrived at Ray's apartment.

And he was ready for her.

He'd stocked a box of condoms in the drawer of his nightstand—just in case. He also had two selections of wine—a nice merlot lying on its side in the pantry, as well as a pinot grigio chilling in the fridge.

Not that he was going to try and seduce her. But this time, he was prepared for a romantic evening, especially since he hadn't been ready the last time.

As he swung open the door, he found her waiting for him, her striking blond hair glossy and curled at the shoulders. She'd chosen a festive red dress for the party, one that was both modest and heart-stopping at the same time.

What other woman could pull off something like that?

The moment their eyes met, all was lost—every thought, every plan, every dream he'd ever had.

What was it about Catherine that had him wishing things were real? That their feelings for each other were mutual? That their engagement wasn't just an act?

"I'm sorry I'm late," she said. "I'd meant to get here sooner."

"No problem." He slipped aside and let her in. "The American Legion Hall is just a short walk from here. We ought to arrive in plenty of time—that is, if you're ready to go."

In the soft living room light, he scanned the length of her one more time, deciding she was as dazzling as ever in that simple red dress and heels.

Yet when he spotted the little black clutch she carried and realized it was too small to hold much of anything, even a toothbrush, a pang of disappointment shot through him.

She'd said that they could talk about the sleeping arrangements later, although he suspected she'd already made up her mind. That is, unless she left an overnight bag in her car—just in case.

A guy could hope, he supposed.

"Do you want to come in for a drink or something?" he asked. "Or do you want to head for the party?"

"I'm ready whenever you are."

"All right, then." He lifted his arm in an after-you manner, then stepped out the door, locked up the apartment and followed her down the stairs.

She looked hot tonight—like a model striding down a runway, all legs and sway. And for the next couple of hours, she was all his.

Another pang of disappointment shot through him. What he wouldn't give to know that she was here because she wanted to be. Would she have come if he'd actually asked her to be his date?

He supposed he'd never know, because he sure wasn't going to ask her.

As they continued out onto the sidewalk and started down Main Street, she slowed in front of the florist shop, where a variety of potted orchids were displayed in the window.

"I love exotic flowers," she said.

He'd have to remember that.

When they reached the beauty shop, which had a Closed sign in the window, Ray came to a stop. "I'm sure you'd never consider getting your hair done in a small town like this, but you ought to check it out sometime. Darla Ortiz, the owner, used to be a Hollywood actress back in the sixties. And she's decorated the place with all kinds of memorabilia."

"No kidding?" Catherine stopped, too, then peered through the window and into the darkened shop that had closed an hour earlier.

Ray caught a whiff of Catherine's floral-scented body lotion, something exotic, something to be handled with care—or cherished from a distance like those orchids at the floral shop.

He did his best to shake it off, as he stood next to her and looked into the darkened hair salon.

"It's pretty cool inside," he said. "Darla has a wall full of framed headshots of various movie stars who were popular forty and fifty years ago. Some are even black-and-whites from the post–World War II era. And each one is autographed to her."

"I'll make a point of stopping by to see them," Catherine said.

Feeling a little too much like one of the older women in town who worked for the local welcoming committee or a fast-talking real estate agent bent on selling the community to a new buyer, Ray said, "Come on. We'd better get moving."

As they started down the street again, he couldn't help adding, "Brighton Valley is a small town with a big heart."

"I've sensed that."

He wanted to say that the same was true of most of the residents, including the mayor, but he decided he'd better reel in his wild and stray thoughts before he went and said something stupid. Something he might not be able to take back.

Instead, he decided to enjoy the evening with Catherine—whatever that might bring.

The Ernie Tucker birthday committee had gone all out in decorating the American Legion Hall for the celebration, complete with red, white and blue balloons and matching crepe-paper streamers. Several picture collages on poster board had been placed at the entrance, as well as in various spots around the room.

Each board had a slew of photographs—old brown and whites, a few Polaroids and some in color. They each provided a view of Ernie's life from the time he was a baby until present day.

"There's a lot of history here," Ray said.

"I can see that."

One particular photograph caught Ray's eye. Ernie was a kid, standing barefoot next to the original Brighton Valley Community Church.

"For example," he said, pointing to the picture. "That church burned down nearly sixty years ago. And the congregation rebuilt it in its present location on Third Street."

"How did it happen?"

Ray chuckled. "Fred Quade and Randall Boswell who, according to my grandmother, never did amount to much, snuck out of Sunday services one summer day. They hid out in the choir room, where they decided to drink a beer and light up a smoke. Before long, they were both sicker than dogs and ran outside, leaving two smoldering cigars next to the robes hanging in the closet. And before long, the church was on fire.

"It seems that old Reverend McCoy was giving one of those fire and brimstone sermons. My grandmother said there were a few people who thought that brimstone was raining down on Brighton Valley."

Catherine smiled, then pointed at a picture of Ernie receiving a Hero of the Year award from the city council back in the 70s. A young boy, Danny Marquez, stood next to him. "Is that Ernie and his son?"

"No, it's the kid whose life he saved. There'd been a car accident, and the vehicle slammed up against a brick building. When it caught fire, the boy was trapped inside. His mother was thrown from the car, but she was seriously injured and couldn't get to her son.

"Ernie came along and, using a tire iron, broke out the front window and pulled him to safety. Ernie suffered some burns in the process, but he became a local hero that night."

"The community must love him." Catherine scanned the crowded room. "Looks like quite of few of them have come out to celebrate his birthday."

"Yep. Ernie has always been one of the white hats, as far as people in Brighton Valley are concerned. Not only was he the town sheriff for nearly forty years, he was also a veteran of World War II and received a Bronze Star. There are a lot of people in town who will tell you that they don't make 'em like Ernie Tucker anymore."

Ray's granddad had been a local hero, too, and if he'd lived to be one hundred, the town would have also come out in droves. But Ray didn't see any need to comment. This was Ernie's big day—and one that was well deserved.

"Come on." Ray nudged Catherine's arm. "Let's go wish ol' Ernie a happy birthday."

They did just that, and for the next two hours, Ray and Catherine made the rounds at the party, talking to one person or another.

Finally, after cake and ice cream had been served, Ray and Catherine wished Ernie the best, then made their way to the door and out onto Main Street.

Just as they were leaving, Kitty Mahoney, one of the local matrons who'd been trying to set him up with her daughter, stopped them and congratulated them on their engagement.

"You're a lucky gal," Kitty told Catherine.

Ray wrapped an arm around Catherine's shoulder. "I'm the fortunate one. I thank my lucky stars every day that this lady agreed to be my wife."

For a moment, he actually believed it—that they truly were a couple, that they had a future together.

Kitty smiled, then went about her way.

Ray loosened his hold on Catherine, letting his hand trail down her back before releasing her altogether. They might have been more affectionate before—the hand-holding, the starry-eyed gazes. But it wasn't so easy pretending anymore, and he wasn't sure why.

He supposed it was because he was having a hard time deciding what was real and what wasn't.

Once they'd stepped outside, where a full moon lit their path, Ray said, "That was probably a boring evening for you, so thank you for being a good sport."

"It wasn't so bad. I've never had the chance to meet a man who was a hundred years old before. That's actually amazing, don't you think? And he seems so sharp."

"He sure is."

They continued their walk down Main Street,

which was fairly quiet, now that the stores had all closed. Yet they weren't doing much talking, either.

Ray wondered if she was pondering the sleeping arrangements—or if she'd already made up her mind.

When their shoulders brushed against each other, he had the strongest urge to reach for her hand—and he might have done it, if she hadn't been holding her small handbag between them.

Was that on purpose? A way to keep her distance?

When they neared the drugstore and the entrance to his apartment, he slowed and nodded toward the front window. "Have you ever been inside?"

"Of the drugstore? No, why?"

"Uriah Ellsworth runs the place, and he just refurbished the old-style soda fountain in back. It's kind of a treat to go in, sit at one of the red-vinyl-covered stools and sip on a chocolate milkshake or a root beer float. I'll have to bring you here one day."

"That sounds like fun."

Did it? Was she enjoying herself in Brighton Valley? Did she have any longing whatsoever to stick around town?

And more important, did she suspect that Ray would like it if she did?

When they reached the stairwell that led to his apartment, Ray slowed to a stop. "Why don't you come up and have some coffee? Or maybe even a nightcap?"

"I'd really like to, but I need to get home. I promised to help Eva work on the girls' costumes for the talent show."

"What girls?"

"Kaylee and her friend Shauna. They created an act, which is pretty good. I choreographed the dance steps for them and have been coaching them."

"No kidding?"

Catherine cocked her head slightly. "What do you find hard to believe? That the girls are actually pretty good? Or that I'm helping them?"

"A little of both, I guess. But I mean that in a good way."

She smiled. And in the golden glow of the streetlight, he could see the pride shining in her eyes. Could he see something else in there, too?

Either way, it didn't seem like something he should put too much stock in. Her feelings—whatever they might be—would only complicate the issue. So he said, "I'm glad you're helping out. It's...a nice thing for the mayor's fiancée to be personally involved in one of the community events. So you can bet I'll be at the talent show, cheering them on."

"Thanks. The girls have really worked hard. I think you'll be pleasantly surprised."

"I already am." And not just about the girls.

He paused for a moment, giving her a chance to change her mind about coming upstairs with him. When she didn't, he said, "Come on, I'll walk you to the parking lot."

They continued to the intersection of Main and First, then they turned left and headed for the alley where she'd left her car.

"You'll never guess what else I'm going to do," she said.

She was full of surprises this evening, it seemed.

"I have no idea," he said. "We haven't had a chance to talk much this past week."

Okay, so maybe that was partly his fault. He'd made a point of not calling her each time he'd thought of her, each time he remembered the night they'd made love.

Her steps slowed as she reached Eva's minivan, and she turned to face him with a bright-eyed smile. "I'm going to help out in the Fine Arts Department at Wexler High School starting next Monday."

She'd been right—he wouldn't have guessed that in a week of Mondays. Maybe he'd been wrong about her hightailing it back to New York and leaving him in the dust. Maybe she was finding her niche in Brighton Valley.

"How did that come about?" he asked, wondering if it meant she had plans to stay in town indefinitely.

"A couple of days ago, Jillian Hollister stopped by the Walker Ranch. I was in the living room, coaching Kaylee and Shauna on their routine. She watched for a while, and then she suddenly lit up and told me that the Wexler High dance teacher is out on maternity leave. Apparently, some of the kids in class had wanted to perform in the talent show, but the substitute teacher they'd brought in has no dancing experience—if you can imagine that."

Actually, he was still trying to wrap his mind around the idea of her taking on a job like that. "So you volunteered to help?" Ray asked.

"Well, when Jillian asked if I'd work with them, I told her I'd be happy to—at least until the night of the talent show."

That was great news. And promising. He liked thinking that she was getting more involved in the community. Maybe she wouldn't be so eager to leave town.

"Sounds like you're settling in," he said.

Settling in?

Oh, *no.* Catherine didn't want him to get *that* idea. Her life, her career, her very identity was in New York. And with *Dancing the Night Away* now a go, she had no reason to stay in Brighton Valley much longer.

Well, no reason other than Ray and the twins she'd come to love. And standing outside with him in the silver glow of a lover's moon, she was almost tempted to reconsider.

Almost.

As she struggled to shake off the sentiment that tempted her to change her course and ruin her chances to ever perform on the Broadway stage again, Ray placed his hand on her back, sending a spiral of heat to her core.

"Are you sure you don't want to spend the night with me?" he asked.

No, she wasn't sure. In fact, she wasn't sure about anything at all right now, especially with that blasted full moon shining overhead and the musky scent of Ray's cologne taunting her with the promise of another wonderful evening spent in his bed.

But if she weakened, then where would she be?

As if he might somehow hold the clue, she looked into his eyes, where the intensity of his gaze dared her to change her mind about staying with him, not only tonight, but in Brighton Valley indefinitely.

Yet how could she give it all up—the dream career, the bright lights, not to mention the culture-rich opportunities in a metropolis she'd grown to love?

As they continued to study each other in silence, his hand remained on her back. He stroked his thumb in a gentle caress, setting her heart on end.

How could such a simple movement be so arousing, so alluring?

She pressed her lips together, forcing herself to remain strong. After a beat, she said, "Staying with you tonight isn't a good idea. My life is in Manhattan. And I'll be going back one day soon. When that happens, it'll be easier if we haven't grown too attached to each other."

His thumb stopped moving, then his hand slowly lowered until he pulled it away altogether. The loss of his touch stirred up a chill in the night air, leaving her to crave his warmth.

And to crave him.

"You're probably right," he said.

Under normal circumstances, she would have been happy to have him agree with her. Yet there was something bittersweet about being right, especially on a night like this.

As they faced each other in the moonlight, Ray reached out again, this time placing his hand along her jaw. His thumb brushed her cheek, warming her once again and deepening her craving for more of him.

"Would it also be a bad idea if I kissed you goodnight?" he asked.

She opened her mouth to tell him yes. But would it be so bad to end their evening together with a kiss?

Oh, for Pete's sake. Her better judgment, which had been battling desire as if her life depended upon it, lost the will to fight any longer and surrendered to temptation.

She slipped her arms around his neck, and with her lips parting, raised her mouth to his. The moment their tongues touched, the memory of their lovemaking came rushing back, making her relive each stroke, each caress, each ragged breath until she was lost in a swirl of heat.

This was *so* not a good-night kiss. Instead, it whispered, *Take me to bed and stay with me forever.*

When they finally came up for air, Catherine's head was spinning.

Really spinning.

She blinked, trying to right her world, yet a burst of vertigo slammed into her. As she grabbed on to Ray to steady herself, her fingers dug into his shoulder. Still, she swayed on her feet.

If he hadn't caught her, she might have collapsed on the ground.

What in the world was happening to her?

"Are you okay?" he asked, humor lacing his voice as if he thought the kiss had a bigger effect on her than it had.

Again, she blinked. Moments earlier, when she'd been kissing him, she'd been so overcome with passion and desire, that she might have described it as head-spinning and knee-buckling. But the buzz she was feeling right now was much more than that.

She was actually dizzy.

Was there any chance she might faint?

"Are you sure you're okay?" he asked again, this time taking her reaction a little more seriously.

As her head began to clear, she managed a smile and tried to downplay whatever had happened. "I guess I lost my head for a moment."

"Me, too. And you can't tell me that's a bad thing."

Sure it was. Losing her head might lead to losing her heart, and that would be a *very* bad thing.

But she wasn't sure where the dizziness had come from. It seemed to be easing now. But was it safe for her to drive home? The winding road that led to the ranch was pretty dark in spots.

"You know," she said, "I'm feeling a little light-headed. I must have eaten something that didn't sit right with me. Maybe I should stay the night."

He brightened. "If that's the case, you shouldn't be driving."

"But I'll sleep on the sofa," she added.

He stiffened, as if her sudden change of course took him completely aback. But then, why wouldn't it? She'd been struggling with her feelings for him ever since the night they'd slept together. And she was still vacillating when it came to knowing what to do about it.

"No," he said, slowly shaking his head. "You take the bed. I'll sleep on the sofa."

"But I'm the one making unreasonable demands," she said.

He placed his hand on her back, disregarding her comment. "Come on. Let's go inside."

She didn't know what he would expect of her once they entered his apartment, but she'd meant what she'd said. She would stay the night, but they wouldn't be sleeping together.

Too bad her hormones were insisting otherwise.

Chapter Ten

Once inside the apartment, Ray told Catherine to sit on the sofa. Then he went into the kitchen, filled a glass with water and took it to her.

He watched her take several sips, all the while checking out her coloring, which was a little pale.

"Are you feeling any better now?" he asked.

She nodded. "That dizzy spell seems to be over. If I wait a little while, I can probably drive home—"

"You're not going anywhere. There's no need to risk driving home in the dark when you can stay here."

She nodded, then glanced down at the glass of water she held. When she looked up, her gaze snagged his. "Thank you, Ray."

"For what?"

"I don't know. Understanding, I guess."

To be honest, he didn't understand any of it—her dizziness, of course. But her reluctance to make love again, when it had been so good between them, confused him. So did her change in attitude toward him, the distance between them, the stilted conversations that had once flowed so smoothly.

What had happened to the old Catherine, the woman he'd hired to be his fiancée, the one who'd at least pretended to hang on his every word and to gaze in his eyes with love?

He'd come to appreciate that woman. Not that he didn't appreciate the new Catherine. He just didn't understand her, that's all.

Was she playing some kind of game with him?

He hoped that wasn't the case.

"Listen," he said. "There's something we need to talk about."

His comment hung in the air for a couple of beats, then she slowly nodded. "You're probably right."

Then why was it so hard to broach the subject, to throw it out there? To encourage her to share her thoughts?

Finally, he said, "I miss the camaraderie we once had."

"So do I. But making love…changed things."

It certainly had. He supposed it always did—no matter who the couple was or what their stories.

"Why do you think that happened?" He had his own ideas, of course. But how did *she* feel about it?

"Because a relationship between us won't work. I mean, your life is clearly in Brighton Valley, and mine is in Manhattan. So even though the sex was incredible—and we seem to…care and respect each other—getting any further involved will only make it difficult for us when I leave."

She had a point, because he would damn sure miss her when she left town. And while it made sense that they protect themselves from getting in too deep, he couldn't help wishing that things could be different. That she would decide to make a life for herself in Texas.

But that was as unlikely as him selling his ranch and moving to New York City.

It would never happen.

"Are you sorry we made love?" he asked.

She smiled, her eyes filling with a sentiment he couldn't quite peg. "No, I don't regret that at all. But I do regret knowing nothing will ever become of it."

The truth in her words poked a tender spot inside him, just like a spur jabbing him in the flanks. And he had to concede that she was right.

"At this point," she added, "we can walk away with a nice memory. But if we get any more involved—or if that involvement is emotional—it might be tough to say goodbye."

It might be tough to do that anyway. But he shook off that thought as well as the implication that she could actually develop feelings for him.

"You've got a point," he admitted. "We don't live in the same worlds."

"If we did, things would be different."

Again the truth she spoke, the reality of the situation in which they'd found themselves, gave Ray another spurlike jab.

If he could come up with any kind of argument, he would have laid it on the table. But there wasn't one to be had.

"I'm glad we got that out of the way," he said. "Now all we have to do is decide on the sleeping arrangements. And like I told you before, I'm taking the sofa."

It had been an easy decision to make—the only one.

Yet three hours later, Ray lay stretched out on the sofa in the living room, trying his best to sleep and not having any luck at all.

She'd told him that she didn't want to risk an emotional involvement with him. And he could see the wisdom in that.

But each time he closed his eyes and tried to drift off, he wondered if he'd already gotten in too deep.

If so, she'd been right.

It was going to hurt like hell when she left town.

Over the next two weeks, Catherine got so caught up at Wexler High School with the talent show rehearsals, as well as with Kaylee and Shauna, that she hadn't been able to spend much time with Ray or go to many of those social engagements he'd been paying her to attend.

Okay, so that was the excuse she'd been giving him.

He didn't seem to mind, though. And that made things easier. After the heart-to-heart chat they'd had the night of Ernie Tucker's birthday dinner, their conversations had been better, but they were still…a bit awkward.

They'd attended the parade in Ernie's honor the next morning, but that afternoon she'd felt a little nauseous and had decided to drive back to the Walker ranch instead of staying over to attend the ice cream social on Sunday.

"I must have picked up a bug of some kind," she'd told Ray, as she got ready to leave the parade. "First the dizziness last night, and now an upset stomach."

"Take care of yourself," he'd said.

And she had. She'd gone straight home, slipped into her nightgown and taken a nap.

The dizziness and nausea had plagued her off and on for a while, although never enough to make her consider calling a doctor. And the busier she kept herself, the better she seemed to feel.

Still, if she didn't kick that bug soon, she'd have to make an appointment with a doctor, and she hated to see someone she didn't know in Brighton Valley. But she'd deal with that if and when the time came.

Now, as she prepared to walk up the stairwell to Ray's apartment, she reached into her purse for the key. She'd told him she'd meet him at his place so they could attend an auction tonight, and she was a little early. But she'd just finished working with the high school dance troupe and couldn't see any reason to drive all the way back to the ranch, then to town again.

She carried a garment bag that held a dress she'd borrowed from Eva, as well as a pair of heels. So she had to transfer everything to one hand so she could fit the key into the lock.

Once inside, she carried her change of clothes to the bathroom, where she would get dressed.

Thirty minutes later, she'd taken a shower and slipped into the light blue dress. Then she'd freshened up her makeup and swept her hair into an elegant twist. By the time Ray arrived, she was ready to go.

"I'm sorry I'm late," he said as he entered the apartment. When he spotted her in the kitchen, pouring herself a glass of club soda, he froze in his tracks. As his gaze swept over her, an appreciative smile stretched across his face. "Nice dress. Is it new?"

"Merely borrowed."

Something borrowed, something blue…

Shaking off the thoughts of the wedding day ditty, she asked, "Did you have a good day?"

"I sure did. And better yet, I heard that Jim Cornwall is doing much better and would like his job back in the not-so-distant future."

She took another sip of her drink, wishing it was ginger ale instead. Her stomach was feeling a little woozy again. "Have I met Jim?"

"No, not yet. He's the elected mayor, the one I've been filling in for."

Oh, that's right. He'd fallen off a ladder while trimming a tree in his yard and had been seriously injured—a skull fracture if she remembered correctly.

Catherine offered Ray a smile. "So that's good news, isn't it?"

"You bet it is. I had no idea how demanding the job would be, especially when it comes to all the social events I have to attend—like this one tonight." Ray nodded toward the bedroom. "Give me a minute, and I'll change clothes. Then we can go."

Catherine didn't have to wait long. True to his word, Ray returned within minutes, wearing a sport jacket and tie. And they were soon in his car and on the way to the Wexler Valley Country Club.

Tonight's event was a dinner and an auction, which would benefit a local Boys and Girls Club that serviced both Brighton Valley and Wexler, the neighboring town.

"You know," she said, as they turned into the country club, "you make a great mayor. And the townspeople really seem to like you."

"Thanks. It's been a good experience. But I'm eager to go back home and be a rancher again."

She could understand that.

Ray parked his SUV in the lower lot, and the two made the uphill walk to the main dining room, where the dinner and silent auction would take place. As he opened the door for Catherine, they were met by the sound of a harpist playing just beyond the entry.

"The music is a nice touch," Catherine said.

"Isn't it?" He smiled, then placed his hand on her back as if nothing had changed between them. "That's got to be Margo Reinhold, the wife of one of our councilmen. She's the only one I know who plays the harp."

They'd no more than entered the main dining room, when Margo's husband approached Ray, taking time to greet Catherine first.

Ray turned to Catherine. "You remember Dale Reinhold, don't you, honey?"

"Yes, I do." She reached out a hand to greet him. "It's good to see you again."

After a little small talk, Dale said, "You heard the news about Jim Cornwall, didn't you?"

"I sure did." Ray lobbed him a bright-eyed grin. "And I'll be counting the days until he comes back."

"Maybe so. But you've been a darn good mayor. You really ought to think about running in the next election."

"Thanks. I'll have to give it some thought."

Catherine had expected Ray to bring up all the work he needed to do on his ranch, but he didn't. Was that because he'd actually enjoyed his stint as mayor?

Either way, she had to agree with Dale. Ray had been doing a great job as mayor. And he was clearly respected by everyone in the community.

As the men continued to talk, a waiter walked by with a tray of hors d'oeuvres—something deep fried and wrapped in bacon. The aroma snaked around Catherine, setting off a wave of nausea.

Oh, dear. Not again. And not here.

"Would you…" She cleared her throat, then issued an "Excuse me" before dashing off to find the ladies' restroom.

Thankfully, just putting some distance between her and the waiter's tray was enough to settle her stomach.

Good grief. What was that all about? Why hadn't she kicked that flu bug?

When she spotted a matronly woman wearing a

tennis outfit, she asked where she could find the nearest restroom and was directed to her left.

Once inside, she found a sitting area and took a seat in an overstuffed chair. Her game plan had been to call a doctor once she got back to New York if she hadn't gotten any better. But maybe she ought to see someone while she was in Brighton Valley. What if the nausea and dizziness were symptoms of something other than a bug, something serious?

If she hadn't already been told that her chances of getting pregnant were slim, she might even wonder about that. But she'd learned a long time ago not to pin her hopes on having a child of her own.

Minutes later, the nausea passed. As she got to her feet, a silver-haired woman entered the room wearing a cream-colored dress and heels. Catherine had met her a time or two, but to be honest, she'd completely forgotten her name or her connection to Ray.

"Well, hello," the woman said. "What a lovely dress. That color really brings out the blue of your eyes."

"Thank you."

"I haven't seen you around lately," the woman added, offering a friendly smile. "It's good to see you and our mayor together."

"I've been busy," Catherine said.

"I heard that." The woman brightened. "You've been helping out with the high school dance group. That's a wonderful thing for you to do. But then again, you are the mayor's fiancée, so it makes sense that you'd jump right in and get involved in the community."

Catherine returned her smile, although she was still at a complete loss when it came to remembering the woman's name. Was she the wife of one of the councilmen?

Maybe she was a councilwoman herself.

"Have you and Ray set a date for your wedding?" the woman asked.

"No, not yet."

"I couldn't wait to set a date when Roger and I became engaged."

Catherine wasn't sure what to say to that.

"June weddings are always nice," the woman added. "Roger and I figured that early summer would be a nice time to take a vacation, if we ever wanted to celebrate our anniversary out of town."

"Now there's a thought."

"Well, all I can say is that you're going to make a beautiful bride."

"Thank you." Catherine fought the urge to check her watch. Ray had to be wondering where she was.

"I hope you plan to have a big wedding."

"Why?" Catherine asked.

"Because everyone in this county loves Ray. And they're going to want to attend so they can wish the two of you their best."

"You're probably right." Catherine offered the woman her sweetest smile, then excused herself and left the bathroom.

She and Ray were going to have to talk about dates all right. Dates for their breakup.

And they'd also need to come up with a good reason for a perfect couple to split and go their own ways.

* * *

Catherine had been fairly quiet all evening, which really shouldn't surprise Ray. She'd been introspective ever since they'd made love. Even the heart-to-heart talk they'd had the other day hadn't made things any clearer.

She'd been right about not getting emotionally involved, but that didn't mean he was happy about the decision to take a step back—no matter what the future might bring.

Ray reached for his steak knife, cut into the filet mignon and took a bite. He'd eaten his share of fancy meals, but he had to admit the chef at the Wexler Valley Country Club had gone above and beyond tonight.

"Are you sure you don't want to have some of my steak?" he asked Catherine.

She'd passed on dinner, choosing only the salad with lemon instead of a dressing. She'd mentioned watching her weight, which he thought was silly. If ever a woman had a perfect shape, it was Catherine. But he decided it wasn't his place to tell her what to eat.

When the people at their table had finished their meals, the wait staff brought out cheesecake for dessert.

"Would you like a bite?" Ray asked Catherine.

"No, thank you."

She certainly had a lot of willpower. Heather, his ex, would have taken her spoon and at least had a taste.

After the waiter picked up the empty dessert plates,

Ray placed his hand on Catherine's. "Are you ready to go, honey?"

"I am, if you are."

He nodded, then stood and pulled out her chair.

One nice thing about these public dinners was being able to pretend that everything was still good between them—even if there really wasn't a "them."

Still, he had to admit that it would have been nice if they really were a couple, if their fake relationship was real. There was something very appealing about being with Catherine, sharing an intimacy he'd never known with anyone else—even if it was all an act.

Would he ever share that kind of relationship with anyone? He hoped so.

Somewhere, deep inside, he was sorry that it might be with a woman he hadn't met, a woman who wasn't Catherine.

After saying their goodbyes to the others at their table, they made their way to the entrance.

"How much money do you think the auction brought in?" she asked.

"Quite a bit. Last year they made ten thousand dollars, and I suspect they did better this time. There had to be at least twenty more people. And they had a lot of nice donations for the silent auction." Ray opened the door, and when he asked Catherine to step outside, she swayed on her feet.

He reached out and grabbed her arm, steadying her. "Are you okay?"

His first thought was that she'd lost a heel or something.

"Yes," she said. "But can we stand here a minute?"

"Sure. Why?"

"I'm a little dizzy again."

His gut clenched. "*Again?* How often have you been having these spells?"

"A few times. Maybe three or four."

He'd been with her on two of those occasions—both of them in the evening. "Where were you when you had the other dizzy spells?"

"Once I was in the bathroom at the Walker ranch. And then it happened again when I was at the high school. But if I sit down for a while, it passes."

He hated the thought of her being sick. "That's a little worrisome, don't you think?"

"I suppose so. But in this case, I didn't eat much for dinner, so maybe that caused me to be a little lightheaded. I probably need to have some protein."

She might be right, but that didn't make him feel much better. What if there was something wrong? Something serious?

"I'll fix you a ham sandwich when we get back to my place," he said.

"That might be too heavy. If you have any cottage cheese, I might have a spoonful."

He never ate cottage cheese, let alone put it on his shopping list. And even if he did, he would insist that she eat more than that.

"I'll tell you what," he said. "Once I get you to the car, I'll go back inside and ask them to put one of those steak dinners in a take-home box."

"Please don't bother the chef with a request like that. I'll find something to eat when we get home."

Home. Just the sound of the word coming from

Catherine's lips made Ray wonder what it would be like if the two of them actually lived together, but given their different ways of life, that would never happen.

"Do you think you can walk to the car now?" he asked.

She nodded. "Yes, let's go."

He slipped an arm around her—just in case she wasn't as steady on her feet as she implied she was—and walked her to the lower parking lot, where he'd left his SUV.

"You're staying with me tonight," he added.

She didn't object, which was good.

The next step was to insist that she make a doctor's appointment first thing Monday morning—whether she wanted to or not.

Once they'd gotten back to Ray's apartment, Catherine gave Eva a call and told her she'd bring the minivan back in the morning.

Ray had insisted that she make an appointment with one of the doctors at the Brighton Valley Medical Center on Monday morning, and she promised to do so—if she had another dizzy spell.

"I'm sure it's nothing to worry about," she added, although she wasn't entirely convinced of that. "I was probably just a little lightheaded from not eating much today."

"Then come into the kitchen with me," he said. "I'll fix you a sandwich."

"All right. But if you don't mind, I'd like you to

leave it open-faced. No mayonnaise, please. And can I please see the nutrition label on that ham?"

He reached for her hand and gave it a warm, gentle squeeze that nearly stole her breath away.

"Okay," he said, letting go. "But you need to understand something. I'm worried about you skipping meals—or relying on rabbit food to keep you going. And while we're on the subject, I'm not sure why in the hell you think you have to diet. You look great."

"I… Well, thank you." She rubbed the hand he'd been holding just moments before. "But just so you know, I've put on ten pounds since arriving. And I don't want it to get out of hand."

She also needed to lose at least that much if she wanted to land the lead role in *Dancing the Night Away,* but she wasn't ready to tell him that.

"You can lose that extra weight without starving yourself." He nodded toward the open kitchen. "Come on. Let's get you some nourishment."

After pulling the ham from the fridge, he handed it over to her to look at the packaging. Then he took a loaf of bread from the pantry.

Catherine read the nutrition label. The deli meat was a low-fat version, so she decided not to stress about it.

Within minutes, Ray had made the sandwich, just the way she'd asked—with one slice of bread and no mayo. He also added some lettuce and tomato, leaving them on the side. Then he carried her plate to the dining area.

"Thanks," she said, taking a seat at the table. "It actually looks pretty good."

"I'm glad." Ray removed his sport jacket, then he carried it into the bedroom, leaving her to eat.

When she'd popped the last bite of the sandwich into her mouth, she took the empty plate back to the kitchen and put it in the sink.

Ray, who'd come out of the bedroom, slipped up behind her. She'd heard him coming, then caught a whiff of his musky aftershave as he placed his hands on her shoulders and slowly turned her around.

"Now that you've eaten," he said, "I have another request."

"What's that?"

His gaze, as intense and arousing as she'd ever seen it, locked onto hers, causing her heart to rumble and her pulse to kick up a notch. But it was the husky tone of his voice and the suggestive words he uttered that nearly dropped her to her knees.

"I want to sleep with you tonight, Catherine."

If she were going to be honest—with him, as well as herself—she would admit that there wasn't anything she'd like better. But making love with him, as star-spinning and mind-boggling as it had been, had left them both on edge around each other. And if she weren't careful, she could ruin whatever friendship they had.

And Ray knew how she felt. He'd even agreed with her.

Of course, that didn't mean she wasn't sorely tempted to make love with him again. And obviously, he was dealing with the same temptation.

The hormones and pheromones that swarmed around them became so strong, so heady, that she could almost see them. But she forced herself to hold steady. "I told you that, under the circumstances, having a sexual relationship wasn't a good idea."

"I said *sleep*. Not make love."

She paused for a beat, thinking about it—and actually liking the idea.

"Even if we don't ever become lovers again," he added, "I'd like for us to be friends. I care about you, Catherine. And I want to share my bed with you."

She cared about him, too. Way more than she dared to admit—to him or to herself. But she would be leaving soon. She'd even purchased her flight back to JFK for the day after the talent show, although she hadn't told Ray yet.

And why hadn't she?

Maybe because she was afraid he had some warped idea that they might actually have a future together. That he'd ask her to stay in Brighton Valley, to be his real fiancée.

If he did, what would she say?

Could she give up her life and her dreams for a man?

Maybe.

And maybe not.

Yet a better question might be: Could she give it all up for Ray? And if so, would she grow to resent him in the long run?

Her heart clamored in her chest, begging to get out and to have a say about it, urging her to agree to more than just sleeping with him, to make love one more time.

And maybe even to cancel her flight back to New York.

But she had to go. And leaving Brighton Valley—leaving *Ray*—was going to be tough enough without running the risk of an emotional attachment, which she feared she already had.

Yet against her better judgment, she said, "Okay. I'll sleep with you."

She told herself she'd made that decision because she hated to have him sleep on the sofa, and she knew he'd insist that she take the bed.

But in truth?

If she was leaving on Sunday, she wanted to sleep next to him tonight.

And even more than that, she wanted to wake up wrapped in his arms.

Chapter Eleven

Ray woke the next morning with Catherine's back nestled against his chest, his arms wrapped around her.

He'd thought that once they'd drifted off to sleep last night, they'd end up on their own sides of the bed, but he'd been wrong. They'd cuddled together until dawn.

As Catherine began to stir, he took one last moment to breathe in the faint floral scent of her shampoo, to relish the feel of her breasts splayed against his forearm.

She turned, adjusting her body so that she faced him, and smiled. "Good morning."

He returned her smile. "'Morning."

"How'd you sleep?"

"Great." Much better than if he'd slept on the sofa, holding on to his pillow. "How 'bout you?"

"Not bad."

"Are you feeling any better?" he asked.

"Yes. I guess I just needed a bite to eat and a good night's sleep."

He hoped so. He'd been worried about her last night.

"Do you want to use the shower first?" he asked.

"All right."

After she climbed from bed, he headed into the kitchen, where he brewed a fresh pot of coffee and searched the fridge for something to make for their breakfast.

He settled on bacon and eggs, although he figured it might be best to ask what she'd like to eat. Maybe she'd rather go to Caroline's Diner.

Minutes later, Catherine entered the kitchen, fresh from the shower.

"Coffee's ready," he said. "Would you like me to make some scrambled eggs? Or would you rather go down to Caroline's? She makes the best cinnamon rolls."

"I'll pass on a big breakfast," she said. "Coffee will be fine for now."

There she went with the dieting again. Hadn't she learned her lesson?

He crossed his arms and leaned his weight onto one leg. "Remember what happened last night? You need more than that to get by on. I don't want you getting dizzy again."

"Okay," she said. "I'll have an egg."

Just one? What was he going to do with her?

Love her came to mind. But he shook off that thought as quickly as it had popped up. All he needed to do was to fall for a woman who was supposed to be leaving town in the near future.

"There's something I need to tell you," she said, taking a seat at the dining room table.

"What's that?" He pulled two mugs from the kitchen cupboard, his back to her as he filled them with coffee.

"I've made plans to return to Manhattan."

His pulse, as well as his breathing, stopped for several beats, and when it started up again, he turned to face her. "When?"

"A week from next Sunday."

Eight short days from now.

"I hope that's okay with you," she added.

Wouldn't it have to be? He'd known it was coming, although it still took him by surprise and left him unbalanced.

"I know we had an agreement," she said, "but the length of it had been indefinite. And, well, I have an opportunity to audition for the lead in a musical, one I'd really like to have."

His heart sank to the pit of his stomach. Not only was she leaving Texas, but she was going back to the life she'd created for herself, the life she loved.

He couldn't fault her for it, but it still…well, it hurt to know she was leaving—and before he was ready to let her go.

Her news had jerked the rug right out from under

his feet, toppling the phony world they'd created for themselves in Brighton Valley.

"We'll have to come up with a reason for our breakup," she added.

It would have to be a damn good one. Everyone in Brighton Valley seemed to like her—and to think of them as a couple. A perfect one at that.

The phony engagement may have worked like a charm, but now he would have to deal with the repercussions of ending it.

Too bad one of those repercussions had just hit him personally like a wild bronc coming out of the chute.

"Are you okay?" she asked.

Hell no. He wasn't okay. But he didn't want her to know that. Or to think that her leaving was going to be any more than a little inconvenience to him. So he glanced at his bare feet, then back up to her face. "I'm sorry, Catherine. I didn't mean to ignore you. I had a couple of things scheduled for later in the month, and I was trying to figure out how I'd manage without you. But you're right. We'll have to concoct a story for everyone—something believable that won't make either one of us look like the bad guy. Can I have some time to think about it?"

"Of course. I'll try to come up with an excuse for our breakup, too."

He handed her a cup of coffee, then grabbed his and took a drink of the rich, morning brew. He hoped the familiar taste, as well as the caffeine, would right his world again.

Three sips later, it hadn't helped a bit.

He'd known this day would come. Why hadn't he

planned for it? Why hadn't he realized they'd need an explanation?

Or *did* they?

Compelled to drag his feet, he asked, "Would it be so bad to let things ride a while?"

"What do you mean?"

"Well… Maybe we can tell people you had to go to take care of business in New York. We can let them think you'll be returning. That would keep the marriage-minded women in town at bay for a bit longer. And by then, maybe Jim will be back on the job as mayor, and I'll be at my ranch more often than not."

She seemed to chew on that for a moment, then began to nod. "That sounds like it might work."

It also bought him some valuable time. Time for Catherine to change her mind about leaving. Or, if she got to Manhattan and missed the small-town life and wanted to return to Brighton Valley, it provided them with an opportunity to pick up right where they'd left off.

At least that's the excuse he seemed to be hanging on to.

What the hell was happening to him? Why the uneasiness about her plans to leave, especially when that had always been part of the plan?

Why was he missing the idea of having her around, when she'd never even hinted that she was looking for a husband or a home, let alone relocating to a town that must seem like Podunk, Texas, after living in a metropolis?

Damn. If he didn't know better, he'd think that he'd fallen in love with another woman who didn't share the same affection for him. And if anyone ought to know better than to imagine a woman having loving feelings where none existed, it was Ray. Heather hadn't placed any value on love, marriage or promises. And when she left the ranch, she'd never looked back.

Of course, Catherine wasn't at all like his ex-wife. She didn't have a selfish or greedy side. At least, not that he'd noticed.

Catherine lifted her cup and took a sip. Then she grimaced and set it down.

"What's the matter?"

"I don't know. It doesn't…taste very good."

"Really? Mine tastes fine." And just the way he liked it, just the way he made it every day.

"I guess it just isn't hitting the spot." She picked up the mug, carried it to the sink, then poured it out. "I'm sorry. I can't drink it."

"Would you rather have some orange juice?"

"I'm not sure. Maybe."

"It would be a lot more nutritious." He strode to the fridge and pulled out the container. "Wouldn't that be better?"

"I think so."

As he poured her a glass, he wondered if she was having any reservations about leaving. Maybe second thoughts, instead of the coffee, had left a bitter taste in her mouth.

Or maybe that was just wishful thinking on his part.

Either way, he was going to have to get used to the idea—no matter how much it weighed him down.

As he handed her the glass of OJ, he thought of

something his grandma used to say: *You don't miss your water until the well runs dry.*

It hadn't been the case for him when Heather had moved out. By then, he'd actually been glad to see her go. But that certainly seemed to be the case now. He felt empty, just at the thought of Catherine going away.

"You know," she said, "if we put our heads together, I'm sure we can think of a good reason for us to break up."

He'd rather come up with a reason for her to *stay.* But she was right. They lived in two different worlds. Forcing her to clip her wings and remain on a ranch or in a small town like Brighton Valley would destroy a part of her—maybe even the part that appealed to him most.

But how was he going to get by without water, now that his well had gone dry?

The night of the talent show finally arrived, and no one was more excited than Catherine. Working with Kaylee and Shauna had been an amazing experience, and so had coaching the Wexler High School students.

Ray had been tied up at a meeting all afternoon, so he told her he'd meet her there and asked her to save him a seat. He'd also mentioned that he had something to talk to her about and suggested she bring an overnight bag so she could stay in town with him.

If her flight had been another week out, she might have refused, fearing that her resolve to leave might weaken. As it was, she'd be flying out of Houston on Sunday afternoon—just a little under twenty-four hours from now.

In all honesty, she was going to miss Ray when she went to New York—more than she'd realized. And certainly more than he would ever know.

So what harm would there be in having one last evening together?

After dressing for the talent show and telling Kaylee she'd see her there, she borrowed one of the ranch pickups and drove to town. Instead of going straight to the theater, she first stopped at the florist shop on Main Street.

Three days ago, she'd ordered two bouquets of red roses to give to her favorite stars after tonight's performances. Wouldn't Shauna and Kaylee be surprised?

Next she drove to the Lone Star Theater, which had been built sixty years ago. When the owner died, his widow hadn't been able to find an investor or a buyer. Upon her death, she donated it to the city.

From what Catherine understood, it wasn't used very often. But it certainly made a perfect place for a talent show, with its old-fashioned curtain, stage and lighting.

Catherine sought a seat in the front section that was reserved for the families of those performing.

Eva and Jane, along with the parents of the younger contestants, had been allowed backstage to wait with the girls. That left Jerald Morrison, Dan and Hank Walker, as well as Kaylee's siblings to sit in the same row as Catherine.

Knowing she would need to get up and present the flowers to the girls, Catherine took an aisle seat, then placed her purse on the one next to it, saving it for

Ray. Rather than hold the flowers and be unable to clap or to read the program, she slipped the bouquets under her chair, where they'd be safe.

Ray, who'd just arrived, greeted the others in the row before slipping into place, next to Catherine. Then he reached for her hand and gave it a squeeze. "Would it be appropriate for me to say 'Break a leg' to the dance coach?"

"Absolutely." She returned his smile.

Moments later, the show began, and Catherine sat back, waiting for the act she hoped would win in the ten-and-under division.

When the time came, and the girls finally stepped onto the stage, looking darling in the costumes Eva had made, Catherine sat upright and leaned forward. Her heart soared at the sight of them, at the smiles on their faces.

Eva and Jane had come around to the front part of the theater and knelt in the aisle, taking pictures. Somehow, even Jerald Morrison had managed to get out of his seat and film the girls using the video camera on his cell phone.

It was nice to see Shauna's new foster family being so supportive of her. The poor kid certainly deserved to finally have a stable, loving home. It was also high time someone recognized how sweet she was, how pretty and talented. And Catherine was thrilled to have the opportunity to encourage her.

As the girls performed on stage, it was clear to everyone that all their practice in the Walkers' living room had paid off. Shauna, who also had a solo part, brought down the house when she belted out the song's refrain.

And no one's heart swelled as much as Catherine's. In a way, she was paying it forward, encouraging young talent to reach their dreams.

When the song ended, Ray rose from his seat, clapping and cheering with all the rest. Yet when his eyes met hers, they seemed to tell her how very proud he was…of *her*.

In all her many performances, going back to those in the high school auditorium, on to college and even those on and off Broadway, no one had cheered like that for her. Sure, she'd been proud of her own success. And so had Jennifer Walker. But it wasn't quite the same as…

Shaking off the sentiment and the memories, Catherine reached for two of the small bouquets she'd set under her chair, but couldn't quite get a grip on them. So she stood and bent over to retrieve them.

The dizziness that had plagued her earlier in the week struck again as she stood upright. But she couldn't miss the chance to offer roses to Brighton Valley's newest and youngest stars. As she headed for the stage, she blinked her eyes, trying to clear her vision.

When she reached the bottom of the stage, she handed one bouquet to Kaylee and the next to Shauna.

"I'm so proud of you two," she said, realizing she would have given anything to have had someone say the same thing to her—and to truly mean it.

The lights up front glared, causing the dizziness to increase. Wanting to find an empty chair in which she could sit until her head cleared, she made her way to the far side of the stage.

In the meantime, Jane Morrison, who was standing in the wings, snapped a photo of the girls holding their roses. The camera's flash set the theater walls spinning.

Oh, God. No, Catherine thought as everything faded to black.

It had taken Ray a moment before he realized that Catherine had disappeared from his vision, and only half that time to see that she'd collapsed on the floor.

He rushed forward, nearly knocking over a couple of parents with cameras. He mumbled an apology, but all he could think of was getting to Catherine. The thought that she was hurt, that she was sick, nearly tore him apart.

When he reached her side, she was just starting to come to.

"What happened?" he asked, his gaze raking over her, trying to assure himself that she was okay.

"I..." She blinked. "When I...bent to pick up those roses...I got a little dizzy. I probably should have asked you to...pass them out for me. But I...wanted to be the one..."

Ray turned to a guy who'd been holding a cell phone, taking a video of the two girls on stage. "Hey, buddy. Will you call an ambulance?"

"Oh, Ray," Catherine said. "Please don't let anyone interrupt the show. If you want me to see a doctor, I will. Can't you take me?"

"Yes, of course." He scooped her into his arms,

holding her close to his chest. The thought of losing her, of…

Hell, if she went back to New York, he was going to lose her anyway, and the truth nearly tore him apart. Because either way, he didn't want to let her go. He…

He loved her came to mind, but he couldn't even consider telling her, not when he knew she was leaving.

The man using his cell phone to film the girls, who Ray now realized was Jerald Morrison, said, "I've got my truck parked right outside the door, Mayor. I'll give you the keys, if you want to take it. I can ride home with my wife."

"Thanks." Ray knew his vehicle was several blocks away, thanks to his late arrival. And he was eager to get her to the E.R. as soon as he could.

"I don't think the girls saw anything," Catherine told Jerald. "But if they did, tell them that I'm fine."

"Don't you worry," he said. "I'll reassure them." Then he reached into his pocket and handed Ray a set of keys. "It's a black Dodge Ram."

Ten minutes later Ray had placed Catherine in the borrowed truck and driven her to the E.R. at the Brighton Valley Medical Center. He parked as close to the entrance as he could.

"I can walk, Ray. The night air has cleared my head. I'm not feeling dizzy anymore."

He agreed to let her give it a try, but he wrapped his arm around her for support and held her close.

Upon entering the two double doors, they headed for a triage area, where they spoke to a nurse. Catherine told her about the fainting spell, the dizziness and the occasional bouts of nausea.

After making note of it, the nurse sent Catherine to the registration desk. There she provided them with the pertinent information, as well as her insurance card.

Fortunately, the waiting room was fairly empty, which was unusual for a Saturday night. But that, Ray realized, could change in a heartbeat.

They chose seats near a television monitor that was set on the Discovery Channel. Catherine seemed to tune in to whatever show was on, but Ray couldn't help thinking about the various diagnoses that they might hear—things like brain tumors, aneurisms…

He supposed it could also be something less scary, like an inner-ear problem. He certainly hoped it was something that minor with an easy fix.

When his cell phone bleeped, indicating a text, Ray read the display and saw that the message was from Dan and read it.

How is Catherine? Dan asked.

So far, so good, Ray texted back. *Waiting to see the doctor.*

Let us know what he says.

Will do.

Kaylee and Shauna won the ten-and-under competition, Dan added. *Both families are thrilled. Please tell Catherine.*

After typing in *OK,* Ray turned to Catherine and gave her Dan's message.

"They won?" A broad smile stretched across her pretty face, lighting her eyes and making her look well and whole again. "I had a feeling they would. They worked so hard."

Ray reached out and caressed her leg. "They did a great job. You did wonders with them."

"Thanks, but it was my pleasure to help out. I really enjoyed watching Shauna come out of her shell. I'm so glad she found a loving home. Jane, her foster mom, has been *so* supportive. And did you see Jerald? He's taking an active paternal role, too. Hopefully, she can remain in the Morrisons' home until she's able to move out and live on her own."

"I hope so, too. The Morrisons raised three kids of their own. When the youngest went to college, they signed up to become foster parents."

While Ray was happy to know about Shauna's good fortune, he couldn't help worrying about Catherine. In fact, he'd been concerned about her ever since she'd had that first dizzy spell on Friday night. And while he hadn't seen her again until this evening, he'd called her every day to ask how she was feeling.

According to Catherine, she hadn't been dizzy since Ernie's birthday dinner. At least, that's what she'd told Ray. And he had no reason to doubt her. But then it had happened again.

Ray glanced at his wristwatch. What was taking so long? He really wanted Catherine to see a doctor.

Twenty minutes later, a tall red-haired nurse called Catherine's name, and Ray got right to his feet.

The nurse let them inside, then took them down one hall and then another. "Here we go," she said as she pulled back a screen and pointed out the hospital exam room assigned to Catherine. "Why don't you take a seat on the bed while I get your vitals."

After taking Catherine's temperature and blood pressure, the nurse checked her pulse, then made note of it on a temporary chart.

"The doctor will be here in a minute or two," she said, before whipping back the curtain and walking off.

That minute stretched out to ten or more. Finally, a lean young man wearing glasses and a lab coat pulled back the curtain and introduced himself as Dr. Mills. He talked to Catherine about her symptoms, then looked at the nurse's notes.

After listening to Catherine's heart and examining her ears, nose and throat, he took a step back. "Everything appears to be normal, but I'm going to ask a lab tech to come in and draw some blood. As soon as I get the results, I'll be back to talk to you."

"Thank you," Ray said.

When the doctor left and they were alone, Ray was finally able to relax long enough to take a seat near Catherine's bed.

"I'm sure it's nothing to worry about," he said, although he wasn't nearly as confident as his words and his voice might imply.

He prayed silently, *God, please don't let it be anything serious.*

Moments later, a balding, middle-age man came in and drew Catherine's blood, then he took the vials to the lab.

To pass the time, Ray tried to make small talk, to

keep both their minds off the possibility that there might actually be something seriously wrong.

Earlier today, when he'd told her to bring her overnight bag and stay with him after the talent show, he'd planned a romantic evening alone. He'd hoped to talk her into making love one more time before she left for New York.

Now, with her health in doubt, he wouldn't think of suggesting sex, which was out of the question. Instead, he'd be content to sleep with her and hold her all night long.

Damn. What was taking so long?

In what seemed like forever, but was less than an hour, the doctor returned.

Catherine, who was sitting on the bed fully dressed, her feet hanging over the edge, bit down on her bottom lip, preparing for whatever news he had to give her.

Ray got to his feet and made his way to her side, taking her by the hand.

"Well," Dr. Mills said, sitting in the swivel chair and wheeling a little closer to Catherine. "I think I have an answer for what's been causing the dizziness and the nausea."

Ray hoped for the best, but braced himself for the worst. Yet nothing prepared him for what the doctor announced.

"You're pregnant."

Chapter Twelve

Pregnant?

Catherine wasn't sure she'd heard him correctly. There had to be some mistake. The other doctor, her gynecologist in New York, had said that it was unlikely she'd conceive, that...

"Are you sure about those results?" Catherine asked Dr. Mills.

"I'm afraid so. You're definitely pregnant, Ms. Loza. And that's probably what's causing you to feel dizzy and nauseous."

Yes, of course. That made sense. But still...

She was pregnant?

Her mind was awhirl. A *baby*. She would have a child of her own, a family...

But what about the upcoming audition? No way

could she consider taking the role, even if they offered it to her.

So what would she do? How would she support herself in New York?

"She's been dieting," Ray told the doctor. "That can't be good for her."

Oh, goodness. *Ray.* Did he realize the baby was his? And if so, how had he taken the news?

She shot a glance his way, saw the seriousness of his expression. But then, why wouldn't he be uneasy? He'd been so stressed about the fact that they'd had unprotected sex, so worried about an unexpected pregnancy.

And now this…

On the bright side, he was still holding her hand. And he hadn't scrunched her fingers in a death grip.

"I don't think the dieting is a problem," Dr. Mills said. "At least, not as long as she starts eating nutritiously from now on. You can ask one of the resident obstetricians about that, but I suspect it's fairly early in the pregnancy. When was your last menstrual cycle?"

"I…" Catherine tried to think. "I guess it's been a while. I've been so busy that I haven't even thought about it."

"She's only about four weeks along," Ray said.

He was right, of course. Catherine, whose mind was still reeling in awe at the news—she was going to have a *baby?*—nodded her agreement. They both knew the exact night it had happened.

"We have several good obstetricians at the Brighton Valley Medical Center," Dr. Mills said. "So if you'd like me to refer you to someone, I can."

But Catherine wouldn't be staying in Brighton Valley.

Of course, if she couldn't dance or act on stage, she had no idea how she'd support herself and a child in New York. Things were horribly expensive there.

Jennifer Walker had faced the same dilemma when she'd gotten pregnant with twins, but Catherine had stepped in to help her out.

When Catherine didn't answer the doctor right away, Ray said, "We'd like you to give us those names."

Surely Ray didn't expect her to stay in Brighton Valley, did he? Supporting herself and a baby here wouldn't be easy, either. What would she do?

Or was he still playing the role of her future husband—just in case word of this got out into the community in spite of all the privacy laws.

Uh-oh. Speaking of their role-playing, what were they going to tell everyone now? "Breaking up" was one thing. But when there was a baby involved? People might not be so understanding of those involved.

Boy, had things gotten complicated.

She and Ray certainly had a lot to talk about, a lot to decide. But he'd paid her to pretend to be his fiancée while she was still in town, so she'd continue to do that, at least until they came up with a breakup plan.

"We won't need those names," she told the doctor.

Ray stiffened, as if she'd somehow challenged him, threatened him. But she hadn't meant to.

"I already know which doctor I'd like to see," she explained. "It'll be Dr. Ramirez, Eva's obstetrician."

Ray relaxed his stance, as well as his grip.

Still, the enormity of the problem facing them was staggering.

"I have to admit," Catherine finally said, "this is quite a surprise for both of us. We're going to have a lot to talk about when we get home."

But where was home? New York? Brighton Valley? Someplace altogether different?

Life as she knew it was over. Maybe not in a bad way, since she was actually thrilled to learn about the baby. But she had no idea how the father-to-be felt about the news.

She shot a glance at Ray, the man who ought to have a say in all of this, the man who was probably going through his own emotional turmoil right now, but she didn't have a clue.

On the other hand, Ray was still trying to wrap his mind around the fact that Catherine was pregnant.

He supposed he'd better thank the good Lord that she was healthy and whole, since that had been his prayer earlier. But she was also expecting his baby.

His baby.

Talk about major dilemmas…

"I'm sure you're right," the doctor said, getting to his feet. "You do have a lot to talk about. I'll finish up the paperwork. Once you check out, you're free to leave."

"Thank you," Catherine said.

Neither of them spoke until after they'd left the hospital and climbed into his car.

"I'm sorry about this," she said.

About what? Getting pregnant?

"Do you plan to keep the baby?" he asked.

"Absolutely. I didn't think I would ever conceive, but that doesn't mean I didn't want a child—or a family."

That was good, wasn't it? He wouldn't have wanted her to consider adoption or anything else. Because even if he didn't have a wife or have any plans to get married again, that didn't mean he never wanted to have any kids.

So that was one hurdle solved.

"I'd like to be a part of the baby's life," he added.

"That might be a little difficult," she said.

Not if she stayed in Brighton Valley.

"Are you still going to leave tomorrow?" he asked.

"I don't know. I'd planned to audition for a part, but if I'm pregnant, there's no way I'll get it."

He wished he could apologize, but he wanted her to stay here. How the heck could he be a part of their child's life if he had to fly back and forth to New York every other month?

"There's a lot to think about," she added.

She had that right. He sucked in a breath, then blew it out again. "Here's something else you ought to consider."

"What's that?"

"We can always get married."

She turned to him, lips parted, as if the suggestion had taken her completely by surprise. Hell, by the look on her face, she'd either been swept off her feet or shocked by the preposterous notion.

But then again, he hadn't expected to propose to her this evening, either. Not when he feared the answer would be no.

"What's the matter?" he asked. "Was the idea too wild for you to even ponder?"

"No, it just took me aback, that's all."

Yeah, well he was a little off-kilter, too. But he didn't like the idea of losing her, especially when he'd be losing his child, too. How was he going to parent a kid who lived in New York?

"You're offering to marry me so the baby has your name?"

For starters, he supposed. He'd kind of like her to have his name, too.

"Marriages should be built on love," she said, "especially if they're meant to last."

"That's true." Sarcasm laced his tone as he thought about the woman who'd promised to love him until death, the woman who'd felt no such thing.

Trouble was, he knew darn well that Catherine wasn't anything like Heather. And he suspected that if she made a commitment to love someone, she would keep it.

But she hadn't said anything about love. And while he'd begun to realize that's what he was feeling for her, he didn't want to lay his heart on the line, then have her throw it right back at him.

Then again, he now had a son or daughter to consider. And he had a chance to have a family again.

"Marriage is still an option," he said. "I care for

you. And I think you have feelings for me, too. To top that off, if we did get married, neither you nor the baby would lack anything. In fact, it might even solve some of our problems."

At least when it came to the phony engagement they'd created, it would help.

"You'd go so far as to marry me?" she asked, the sadness in her voice leaving him a bit unbalanced.

Did she think marrying him was a step down from what she deserved? Heather certainly had.

"Do you want to be a single mother?" he asked.

"At this point, I really don't mind. I'm actually glad to know that I was able to conceive. Being unwed and pregnant doesn't have the stigma it once did."

Maybe not. But what were all the townspeople going to think when they learned that Ray had fathered a baby and didn't marry the child's mother, especially when the woman was one who'd charmed her way into their hearts within a matter of weeks?

And it wasn't just the townspeople he worried about. His parents and grandparents would rise from their graves and haunt him like crazy if he didn't do the right thing by the woman he...*loved.* What was he going to do without her? Just thinking about losing her hurt like hell.

But what options did he have? He couldn't hire Catherine to be a *pretend* wife.

"It's really not a big deal," she added.

Oh, no? It seemed like a very big deal to him. After all, the woman he loved was taking his child and leaving him. And that hurt far more than anything Heather had ever said or done to him.

"I guess we can talk about it more when we get home," he said.

Silence stretched between them for a mile or two, and as he neared Main Street, she said, "You know what? I'm really exhausted. I'd like to go back to the ranch tonight. Would you mind dropping me off at the theater? I left Dan's truck there."

"I thought we had a lot to talk about."

"It might be better to sleep on it and talk tomorrow."

He glanced across the console at her, only to see her looking out the passenger window, her thoughts as far from him as the mountain in the distance.

What had happened? What was bothering her?

Ray was tempted to ask, but hell. He'd already had one city woman turn on him. What made him think Catherine wasn't doing the same damn thing?

He'd been down that painful road before. And he knew how badly things could end when two mismatched people said "I do."

But were they really mismatched and destined for heartbreak?

He wished he could say for sure. And while he was tempted to ask her to reconsider, he wouldn't.

The only thing worse than losing the love of his life would be chasing after her and begging her to stay when she was dead set on leaving.

So after dropping Catherine off at Dan and Eva's, he walked her to the door. Instead of the goodbye kiss he'd been tempted to give her, if she'd seemed to be willing, he gave her something to think about instead.

"No matter what happens, I want you to know that

I'm happy about the baby. The pregnancy might have blindsided me, but I'm getting used to the idea of being a father. And no matter what you decide, I want to be a part of the baby's life."

"That might not be easy."

"Yeah, well, sometimes the best things in life are worth fighting for."

She seemed to think about that for a moment, then said, "Thanks, Ray. That helps."

He hoped so, because it certainly hadn't seemed to help him.

"Good night," he said. "I'll talk to you in the morning."

Then he climbed into Jerald Morrison's truck, which he was going to have to return tomorrow, and drove back to his ranch.

Still, as he entered the empty, sprawling house, he was glad to be home, the memory-filled place where he'd grown up.

It was odd, he thought. When he and Heather had split, and she'd left him alone in this house, he hadn't been swamped in memories of childhood, of fishing with his grandpa or riding fence with his dad.

Instead he'd been angry and driven to shake every last thing that reminded him of her, every dream he'd ever had, every memory he'd ever cherished.

If it came right down to it, he might have run for city councilman as a way to get off the ranch, to shake the reminder of a marriage gone bad.

But Catherine had changed all that. And now, walking through the living room, where his mother used to sit with her knitting needles, crocheting baby blankets for the various expectant mothers she knew from church, Ray remembered it all.

And he missed it more than he'd ever thought possible.

Why was that?

What had Catherine done to him?

Somehow, in the midst of all the playacting, the pretending, he'd found the love of his life. Thanks to Catherine, he'd shaken all the anger, all the bad memories. And he was ready to reclaim all that had once been good and right.

As he climbed the stairs and headed for his bedroom, he wondered if he'd ever have a loving marriage with a woman who would stick by him through thick and thin.

As much as the dilemma perplexed him, he couldn't help wanting to make things right with Catherine—and by that, he meant making them real.

After Ray had dropped Catherine off at the ranch, Eva and Dan met her at the front door, worry sketched across their faces.

"Are you okay?" Eva asked. "What did the doctor have to say?"

Catherine might have kept the news to herself, but she'd been alone and on her own for so very long that she needed to confide in someone. And Dan and Eva were more like family to her than her many siblings.

"I'm not sure how Ray will feel about me telling you this," Catherine began, "especially so soon, but…" She took a deep, fortifying breath, then slowly blew it out. "I'm pregnant."

Dan blinked and cocked his head, as if he'd been as surprised by the news as she'd been.

But Eva, who'd known that Catherine hadn't expected to have a baby of her own, even though she'd secretly longed for one, wrapped her in a warm embrace. "I'm so happy for you."

"Thanks."

As Eva slowly lowered her arms, she gazed into Catherine's eyes. "You *are* happy about the baby, aren't you?"

"Yes, of course I am. But it certainly complicates things."

"Does it change your plans to leave?" Dan asked.

"It changes *everything*—and in ways I can't quite comprehend right now." Catherine blew out another heavy sigh.

"How does Ray feel about it?" Eva asked.

"He's taking it pretty well—at least for a man who went so far as to hire a fiancée so the single women in town would realize he wasn't interested in love or romance."

"Sounds like he wasn't too down on the *romance* part," Dan said with a grin.

Eva gave her husband a little elbow jab, as if his humor might not be appreciated. But it's not as though there'd been any seduction going on. They'd both been willing.

"It just...well, it just happened," Catherine said. "Neither of us planned on..."

What? Falling in love?

She certainly hadn't expected a feeling like that to develop. And what made it worse was that Ray had never given her reason to believe that he was feeling the same way about her.

Sure, he'd suggested marriage. But she'd be darned if she'd marry someone just because it was the honorable thing to do.

If he'd told her that he loved her, if he'd been sincere, she might have considered accepting his proposal. But she couldn't get involved with another man who didn't love her. And she couldn't "pretend" that a wedding ring was the solution to their problem.

Speaking of rings, she glanced down at her left hand, at the heirloom Ray had loaned her to wear. She'd have to give it back to him before she left town. That is, if she left.

What was she going to do?

"Maybe I should put on a pot of chamomile tea," Eva said. "It sounds as if you might need it after all you've been through this evening."

As much as Catherine would like to have a confidant tonight, a woman who would understand why she couldn't accept Ray's proposal—if you could call it that since it had merely been a suggestion—she wanted to retreat to her bedroom, where she might be able to come up with a game plan she could live with.

"Thanks, Eva. But I'm really tired. It's been a taxing day and evening. And what I really need is a good night's sleep."

But even after Catherine had shed her clothes, put on a nightgown and climbed into bed, sleep had been a long time coming.

And morning arrived too soon.

* * *

Ray waited until nearly seven o'clock before driving to the Walkers' ranch. It was probably way too early for a Sunday morning visit, but he didn't want to wait much longer. Catherine was still holding a ticket for a flight leaving this afternoon, and he didn't want her to go before he had a chance to tell her what he had to say.

Last night, while he'd tossed and turned, thinking about what all he stood to lose, he realized that he hadn't told Catherine how he'd come to feel about her. She might throw it right back at him, but it was a risk he had to take.

What if she left and he'd never told her how he felt? Would he regret it for the rest of his life? After all, what were the odds that he'd meet another woman who would touch his heart the way Catherine had?

Probably slim to none.

So he parked Jerald's pickup near the Walkers' barn, then made his way to the front door and knocked.

Kevin, who was still in his pajamas, answered. "My dad already went out to the barn. You can find him there."

Ray figured as much. Ranchers didn't lollygag over coffee, even on Sundays. "Actually, Kevin, I came to talk to Catherine. Is she here?"

"I think she's still asleep. Want me to wake her up?"

"Sure. Go ahead."

Ray took a seat on the sofa, but he didn't have to wait long. Catherine came into the living room just moments later, wearing a light blue robe over a white cotton gown. Her hair was tousled from sleep, and her feet were bare.

Ray stood, then nodded toward the door. "I need to talk to you. Do you mind going out on the porch with me?"

She fiddled with the lapel of her robe for a moment, then said, "All right."

As Catherine followed Ray outside, she couldn't imagine what he had to say. Would he bring up marriage again? Or maybe ask her to stay in town and give up her career?

She might have to do that anyway, although now, with a baby on the way, performing on Broadway had lost some of its appeal. Besides, she'd like to be near family when the baby came. And Dan and Eva, who'd become so much more than friends to her, held that place in her heart.

Maybe she could find her niche in a small town. She'd enjoyed working with the kids… And there was a theater that wasn't used nearly as much as it ought to be.

But that was wishful thinking. Ray didn't love her. And he didn't really want a wife. So how could she consider staying, especially when people learned she was carrying the mayor's illegitimate baby?

Once the door to the house was closed, and they were standing on the porch, Catherine asked, "What did you come to say?"

"Something I should have told you last night."

"What's that?"

He waited a beat, then said, "I may have hired

you to be my fiancée, but along the way, I fell in love with you, Catherine. And I should have told you that when I suggested we get married. I liked the roles we played. And I'd want them to be real."

She liked being with Ray, too. And she'd even begun to like the woman she'd pretended to be, thinking that might be the person who lived deep within. But did she dare hope… Did she dare believe…

"You *love* me?" she asked, trying to wrap her heart and mind around his confession, needing to hear him say it again, wanting to believe him.

"Yes, I love you. And even if that doesn't make any difference to you, I wanted you to know."

"Why didn't you say anything last night?"

"Because I couldn't believe a woman like you would love a guy like me. And with you leaving…"

"You *love* me?" she repeated. That was even more amazing than finding out they were having a baby.

He smiled, and a glimmer lit his eyes. "I think I fell for you the first day I saw you and spotted all those stickers on your face."

"You're kidding. I think that's when I started falling for you, too."

He cocked his head slightly, his smile fading into seriousness. "Are you saying that you feel the same way about me?"

"Yes, Ray. I love you, too."

He let out a whoop that might surprise any of his conservative constituents. "Then it looks like we've pretty much worked through all the complications that matter."

That was true. And she was beginning to believe

that she could finally have it all—marriage to the man she loved, a wonderful father for her baby, the family she'd always wanted.

"So does that mean you'll marry me?" he asked.

"If you're asking me again, then I'm saying yes this time around. There's nothing more in the world I want than to be your real wife and the mother of our baby."

Then she wrapped her arms around him and kissed him with all the love in her heart.

The love they professed, the love they felt, was the real deal—and it promised to be the kind to last a lifetime.

* * * * *

**COMING NEXT MONTH from Harlequin
Special Edition®**
AVAILABLE JUNE 19, 2012

#2197 THE LAST SINGLE MAVERICK
Montana Mavericks: Back in the Saddle
Christine Rimmer

Steadfastly single cowboy Jason Traub asks Jocelyn Bennings to accompany him to his family reunion to avoid any blind dates his family has planned for him. Little does he know that she's a runaway bride—and that he's about to lose his heart to her!

#2198 THE PRINCESS AND THE OUTLAW
Royal Babies
Leanne Banks

Princess Pippa Devereaux has never defied her family except when it comes to Nic Lafitte. But their feuding families won't be enough to keep these star-crossed lovers apart.

#2199 HIS TEXAS BABY
Men of the West
Stella Bagwell

The relationship of rival horse breeders Kitty Cartwright and Liam Donovan takes a whole new turn when an unplanned pregnancy leads to an unplanned romance.

#2200 A MARRIAGE WORTH FIGHTING FOR
McKinley Medics
Lilian Darcy

The last thing Alicia McKinley expects when she leaves her husband, MJ, is for him to put up a fight for their marriage. What surprises her even more is that she starts falling back in love with him.

#2201 THE CEO'S UNEXPECTED PROPOSAL
Reunion Brides
Karen Rose Smith

High school crushes Dawson Barrett and Mikala Conti are reunited when Dawson asks her to help his traumatized son recover from an accident. When sparks fly and a baby on the way complicates things even more, can this couple make it work?

#2202 LITTLE MATCHMAKERS
Jennifer Greene

Being a single parent is hard, but Garnet Cottrell and Tucker MacKinnon have come up with a "kid-swapping" plan to help give their boys a more well-rounded upbringing. But unbeknownst to their parents the boys have a matchmaking plan of their own.

You can find more information on upcoming Harlequin® titles, free excerpts and more at www.HarlequinInsideRomance.com.

HSECNM0612

REQUEST YOUR FREE BOOKS!

2 FREE NOVELS PLUS 2 FREE GIFTS!

◆ Harlequin®

SPECIAL EDITION

Life, Love & Family

Harlequin®

SPECIAL EDITION

Life, Love and Family

USA TODAY bestselling author

Leanne Banks

begins a heartwarming new miniseries

Royal Babies

When princess Pippa Devereaux learns that the mother of Texas tycoon and longtime business rival Nic Lafitte is terminally ill she secretly goes against her family's wishes and helps Nic fulfill his mother's dying wish. Nic is awed by Pippa's kindness and quickly finds himself falling for her. But can their love break their long-standing family feud?

THE PRINCESS AND THE OUTLAW

Available July 2012!
Wherever books are sold.

This summer, celebrate everything Western with Harlequin® Books!

www.Harlequin.com/Western

HSE65680

*Harlequin® American Romance® presents a
brand-new miniseries* HARTS OF THE RODEO.

*Enjoy a sneak peek at AIDAN: LOYAL COWBOY
from favorite author Cathy McDavid.*

Ace walked unscathed to the gate and sighed quietly. On
the other side he paused to look at Midnight.

The horse bobbed his head.

Yeah, I agree. Ace grinned to himself, feeling as if he,
too, had passed a test. *You're coming home to Thunder
Ranch with me.*

Scanning the nearby vicinity, he searched out his mother.
She wasn't standing where he'd left her. He spotted her
several feet away, conversing with his uncle Joshua and
cousin Duke who'd accompanied Ace and his mother to the
sale.

He'd barely started toward them when Flynn McKinley
crossed his path.

A jolt of alarm brought him to a grinding halt. She'd
come to the auction after all!

What now?

"Hi." He tried to move and couldn't. The soft ground
pulled at him, sucking his boots down into the muck. He
was trapped.

Served him right.

She stared at him in silence, tendrils of corn-silk-yellow
hair peeking out from under her cowboy hat.

Memories surfaced. Ace had sifted his hands through
that hair and watched, mesmerized, as the soft strands
coiled around his fingers like spun gold.

Then, not two hours later, he'd abruptly left her bedside,
hurting her with his transparent excuses.

She stared at him now with the same pained expression she'd worn that morning.

"Flynn, I'm sorry," he offered lamely.

"For what exactly?" She crossed her arms in front of her, glaring at him through slitted blue eyes. "Slinking out of my room before my father discovered you'd spent the night or acting like it never happened?"

What exactly is Ace sorry for? Find out in
AIDAN: LOYAL COWBOY.

Available this July wherever books are sold.

Harlequin *Super Romance*

Debut author

Kathy Altman

takes you on a moving journey
of forgiveness and second chances.

One year after losing her husband in Afghanistan,
Parker Dean finds Corporal Reid Macfarland at her
door with a heartfelt confession and a promise to save
her family business. Although Reid is the last person
Parker should trust her livelihood to, she finds herself
captivated by his silent courage. Together,
can they learn to forgive and love again?

The Other Soldier

Available July 2012 wherever books are sold.

HSR71790

Harlequin® *Romance*

A secret letter…two families changed forever

Welcome to Larkville, Texas, where the Calhoun family has been ranching for generations. When Jess Calhoun discovers a secret, unopened letter written to her late father, she learns that there is a whole other branch of her family. Find out what happens when the two sides meet….

A new Larkville Legacy story is available every month beginning July 2012.

Collect all 8 tales!

www.Harlequin.com

HR17818CONT